SICK
— OF —
SHADOWS

MARION CHESNEY

St. Martin's Paperbacks

For my sister, Matilda Chesney-Grenier,
with love and many thanks
for all the Edwardian research books

This is a work of fiction. All of the characters, organizations and events portrayed in this novel are either products of the author's imagination or are used fictitiously.

SICK OF SHADOWS

Copyright © 2005 by Marion Chesney.

Library of Congress Catalog Card Number: 2004051358

ISBN: 0-312-99800-7
EAN: 9780312-99800-4

Printed in the United States of America

St. Martin's Press hardcover edition / August 2005
St. Martin's Paperbacks edition / November 2006

St. Martin's Paperbacks are published by St. Martin's Press, 175 Fifth Avenue, New York, NY 10010.

10 9 8 7 6 5 4 3 2 1

ONE

✠

The aristocracy lived in a closed world protected by a shell of wealth and title, as hard and as glittering as a Fabergé egg. The vast outside world of England where people could die of starvation barely caused a ripple in their complacency.

Then, horror upon horrors, the unthinkable happened. A Liberal government was elected, proposing old-age pensions and health insurance and other benefits for the lower classes. They further proposed eight-hour days, workers' compensation, free school meals and free medical services. Even that aristocrat, young Churchill, had turned Liberal and was saying, "We want to draw the line below which we will not allow persons to live and labour."

With a few exceptions, the aristocracy closed ranks as never before. The old idea that the House of Commons was an assembly of gentlemen had passed.

Admittedly these winds of change were at first regarded as irritating draughts, such as were caused when a lazy footman had left the door of the drawing-room open. But with the newspapers heralding the reforms every morning, high cultured voices could be heard exclaiming over the grilled kidneys at breakfast tables. "Who is going to pay for all this? Us, of course."

Many blamed the fact that free elementary education had been introduced in 1870. The lower classes should not have been taught to think for themselves.

So the aristocracy hung grimly onto the snobberies and rules of society which kept the hoi polloi outside.

But the Earl and Countess of Hadfield felt that the enemy was within the gates in the form of their daughter, Lady Rose Summer, who had cheered the result of the election. At first they thought she had reformed. She had become engaged to Captain Harry Cathcart. Admittedly it could be said that the captain was in trade because he ran his own detective agency, but he came from a good family and had enough money to support their daughter in the style to which she was accustomed.

Nonetheless the couple showed no sign of setting a date for the wedding, nor, for that matter, did they see much of each other.

Rose's parents did not know that her engagement was one of convenience, thought up by the captain to prevent Rose being shipped off to India with the other failed débutantes.

Then Rose had made a companion out of Daisy Levine, a former chorus girl whom she had first elevated to the position of maid and then to that of companion.

Rose, with her thick brown hair, delicate complexion and large blue eyes, was still considered a great beauty, but she repelled men with her encyclopaedic knowledge and radical ideas.

Her parents would have been amazed, however, if they

had guessed that Rose went to considerable pains to please them. She suffered seemingly endless days of parties and teas and calls and balls, all of which bored her, but she felt she owed her parents some dutiful behaviour for having failed at her first Season and cost them a great deal of money.

One evening in late spring, Rose and Daisy were preparing to attend yet another ball. Rose was relieved because on this one rare occasion the captain had promised to escort her. This would be at least one evening free from the pitying looks and sniggers of the débutantes who kept asking slyly where her fiancé was.

It was an even more boring life for her companion, Daisy. Daisy, like Rose, was barely twenty, and yet she was not expected to dance and was condemned to sit and watch with the other companions.

And then, half an hour before they were all due to depart for the Duke of Freemount's ball, Harry Cathcart telephoned to say that an urgent case had come up and he could not be there. Folding her lips into a thin line, Lady Polly, Rose's mother, asked the earl's secretary to telephone Sir Peter Petrey to come immediately and escort Rose. Peter was a willowy effete young man who specialized in filling in at dinner parties when someone had cancelled at the last minute and escorting ladies to balls whose escorts had failed to turn up. He was handsome with thick fair hair and a lightly tanned face.

Lady Polly suppressed a sigh when she saw him. Why couldn't Rose have picked someone like that? The unworldly Lady Polly did not know that Peter had no sexual interest in women at all, her lack of knowledge in sexual matters being hardly surprising in this Edwardian era where an eminent surgeon had declared that no lady should ever enjoy sex—only sluts did that.

3

"Where is the wretched man?" asked Peter as he led Rose up the grand staircase at the Freemounts' town house.

"Working, I suppose," said Rose.

"My dear, a beauty like you should never have involved yourself with a chap in trade. There, now. That was too, too wicked of me. But were you mine, I would never leave your side."

Rose's companion had put her mistress wise to Sir Peter and so Rose smiled amiably and accepted the compliment. She often toyed with the idea of marrying Peter. It would be an arranged marriage, of course, but that way she would have her own household and be spared the labour of producing a child every year.

Rose curtsied to her hosts and entered the ballroom. "With Peter again," she heard the duchess say loudly. "Too sad."

Her voice carried. With so many of the aristocracy hard of hearing because of blasting away at birds and beasts with their shotguns, the duchess, like so many, spoke in a high clipped staccato voice which carried right cross the ballroom.

Rose usually derived some comfort from being the most beautiful lady in the ballroom. But that evening, she was eclipsed.

A new arrival to society was pirouetting around the floor on the arm of a besotted guardsman. She had masses of thick blonde hair woven with tiny white roses. Unlike Rose's slim figure, hers was of the fashionable hourglass variety, with a generous white bosom displayed by the low cut of her evening gown. Her eyes were enormous in her heart-shaped face and of a deep brown, which contrasted seductively with her fair hair and perfect skin.

Daisy, sitting next to an elderly dowager, Countess Slerely, whispered, "Who's the new beauty?"

The countess raised her lorgnette and then lowered it. "Oh, that. That is Miss Dolly Tremaine. Her father is only a rector. She really has nothing more than her looks to recommend her. I'm afraid she'll have to marry someone very old. All the young men want money. Where is Lady Rose's fiancé?"

"Coming later," lied Daisy.

"Most odd. For her sake he should really stop being a tradesman."

"Being a detective isn't really trade," said Daisy defensively.

"The only trades that are acceptable," declaimed the countess, "are tea and beer. Nothing else."

Daisy sighed. Her stays were digging into her and the ballroom was too hot.

She rose and curtsied to the countess and made her way to the long windows which overlooked Green Park, slid behind the curtains, opened the window and let herself out onto the terrace and took a deep breath of sooty air. She wondered if she and Rose would ever have any adventures again.

Rose was making her way to the cloakroom. One of her partners had trodden on her train and ripped the edge of it. The maid on duty in the cloakroom set to work to repair the train. The door opened and Dolly Tremaine came in, tears pouring from her eyes.

"My dear," exclaimed Rose. "May I help you? What is the matter?"

"Nothing," sobbed Dolly, sitting down on a chair next to Rose. "I'm tired, that's all. So many balls and parties. I never seem to get any rest. The Season begins next week and things will be worse."

"If I can be of any help . . ."

"I need a friend," said Dolly, scrubbing at her eyes with a lace handkerchief. Rose noticed with surprise that her beautiful face now bore no mark of tears.

"Perhaps I may be your friend. I am Rose Summer."

"I'm Dolly Tremaine. You see, I'm a country girl and everything in London is so big and noisy and frightening."

"I get away from it in the mornings," said Rose. "I go out early and cycle in Hyde Park."

"I would love to do that," said Dolly, "but I don't think my parents—"

She broke off as the door opened and a squat woman entered. She was wearing a purple silk gown trimmed with purple fringe. Rose thought she looked like a sofa.

"Dolly, what are you doing here?" she demanded.

"My train was torn and this lady came with me to see if she could help," said Rose quickly.

"Why? That's what maids are for. Who are you?"

"I am Lady Rose Summer," said Rose haughtily.

The change in the woman was almost ridiculous. "How kind of you to look after my little Dolly," she gushed. "I am Dolly's mother."

"I was just inviting your daughter to go cycling with me in Hyde Park tomorrow morning," said Rose.

"Oh, I'm sure she would love that but, alas, she does not have a bicycle."

"I will supply one," said Rose grandly. "Furnish me with your direction and I will send a carriage for your daughter— at nine o'clock, say?"

"You are so very kind. Here is my card. Come, Dolly. Lord Berrow is waiting for you."

She turned away. Dolly meekly followed.

6

"But that's my bicycle!" protested Daisy when she and Rose were being made ready for bed. "The captain gave it to me!"

"It's only one morning, Daisy," said Rose. "I would like to do something for that poor girl. I think she is being bullied by her mother."

"You're bleedin' jealous cos she's prettier than you," said Daisy, "and you're trying to cover it up by being nice to her."

"Go to bed, now!" commanded Rose. "Let me hear no more about it."

Ever since Rose had fallen from grace by attending a suffragette movement rally and had been banned from going anywhere near that organization, she had longed to do something for somebody, and so she set out for Hyde Park the following morning on her bicycle followed by two footmen, one of them wheeling Daisy's bicycle. She was determined to find out what had made the beautiful Dolly so sad. Deep down inside her she was motivated by the petty thought that she'd better show society she was above jealousy, but that thought did not even reach as far as her brain.

Nine o'clock was considered an early hour of the day to members of society. Rose would have gone to the park earlier, say six o'clock, had she been allowed to do so. There was something exciting about being up at dawn in a great city and feeling it coming alive with the restless clatter of traffic, the whinnying of horses, and the air briefly fresher before the thousands of London's coal fires put a thin haze over the sun, even on a fine spring day, and streaked the buildings with soot.

As she approached the Serpentine, one of the earl's carriages drove up. A footman jumped down from the backstrap and let down the steps. Dolly tripped prettily down them. She was wearing a white lace gown with a high-boned collar and a round straw hat covered in white flowers. Worn open over her gown was a fur-trimmed coat. On her feet were little white patent leather boots.

"Oh, my dear Miss Tremaine," exclaimed Rose. "You should have worn a divided skirt. You cannot cycle in such clothes."

Dolly burst into tears. "I—I'm always doing something wrong," she sobbed.

"There, there," said Rose, patting her awkwardly on the back. "Do dry your eyes. We shall walk instead." She surrendered her bicycle to one of the footmen. "Now, do try to be cheery. It is too fine a morning to be sad."

Dolly complied and took Rose's arm, a gesture Rose felt was a trifle over-familiar. She drew her arm away. Dolly began to cry again. "I've offended you!"

"No, no. Please sit down on this bench. Do compose yourself. Why are you so distressed?"

"I don't know the rules," sniffed Dolly. "So many rules. We were taking tea yesterday at Mrs. Barrington-Bruce's place in Kensington. Such a splendid tea and I have a healthy appetite. I ate an awful lot and then I found the other ladies were looking at me in horror. Worse than that, I'd taken off my gloves. I did not know one was supposed to eat with gloves on."

"Usually the form is to eat only a little thin bread and butter," said Rose. "It is rolled, you see, so that one does not get butter on one's gloves."

"I talk an awful lot about the country because I do miss it

so," said Dolly, "and Mother says they are all laughing at me and calling me the Milkmaid."

"I think it would be a good ploy if you were to say as little as possible. Just look enigmatic."

"What does that mean?"

"Mysterious. Hidden depths."

"But the gentlemen can sometimes make very warm remarks and I am fearful of offending them."

"Let me see. You rap the offender lightly on the arm with your fan and lower your eyes and say something like, 'Oh, sir, I fear you are too wicked for me. But perhaps I am naïve. I shall tell Mama exactly what you have just said.' Believe me, that will cool their ardour."

"You are so, so clever! Tell me more."

Flattered and feeling she was finally being of use to someone, Rose went on to help her pupil further.

But the morning was rather spoilt for her when, just before she left, Dolly said, "I would like to meet your fiancé. He seems to be a most fascinating man. But people do say he is never at your side."

"People talk a lot of nonsense," retorted Rose angrily.

Daisy was waiting for Rose when she returned. "You look cross," commented Daisy. "What did she do to upset you?"

"Nothing. She is a delightful and charming innocent. I was able to give her some tips as to how to go on in society. We shall meet again. She does cry a lot. She is very sensitive."

"Probably acting," sniffed the jealous Daisy. "Well, if she didn't make you cross, who did?"

"It's just that people are constantly harping on about my supposed fiancé and wondering why he is never with me.

9

I really did think the captain would keep up some sort of pretence."

"Then let's go and see him," said Daisy eagerly. "There's no harm in calling on a fellow in his office."

"I would not *lower* myself to go and beg him."

"But—"

"No more, Daisy."

I'm supposed to be her companion and friend, thought Daisy sulkily, but she still talks down to me. Then her face brightened. She had a soft spot for the captain's manservant, Becket. She would call on Becket. He would know what to do.

"Do you need me for anything?" asked Daisy.

"I don't know. What appointments do we have for today?"

"This afternoon you've to make calls with your mother. You won't need me."

"I suppose not. What will you do?"

"Dunno. Look at the shops."

"Don't say dunno," admonished Rose, but Daisy affected not to hear her and left the room.

As the day was fine, Daisy walked from Belgravia to Chelsea and to Water Street, where the captain had his home. Her heart beat a little more quickly under her stays as she turned the corner of Water Street. It seemed ages since she had last seen Becket. She imagined his surprise when he opened the door and saw her standing there.

But to her dismay, it was Captain Harry Cathcart himself who answered the door. Daisy always found him rather intimidating. He was a tall man in his late twenties with black hair already greying at the temples and a hard handsome face with deep black eyes under heavy lids.

"Where's Becket?" asked Daisy.

"I am afraid Becket is not well. He has a severe cold and I have sent him to bed. Is that why you came? Do come in."

Daisy followed him into the book-lined front parlour. "Do sit down, Daisy."

"You've to call me Miss Levine," said Daisy with a show of spirit. "I'm a companion now. I'm worried about Rose."

"Why? What's the matter?"

"You're supposed to be her fiancé, but you're never seen with her and people are sniggering and talking. She goes everywhere with that Sir Peter Petrey and people are thinking she might ditch you for him."

"Petrey? He has no interest in women."

"You know that, I know that, Rose knows that, but look at it from her point of view. She could marry him and have her own household and not have to worry about producing children. Why should she stick with you?"

"Daisy—Miss Levine—you know very well that our engagement is merely an arrangement. I have been very busy. Well, I suppose I have been remiss. Where does she go this evening?"

"Another ball. The Barrington-Bruces."

"Tell her I will escort her."

"Tell her yourself. She don't know I'm here and she would be furious if she found out. May I see Becket?"

"He has a bad cold and you should not be visiting gentlemen in their bedchambers."

"Just a quick word," pleaded Daisy.

She expected Becket's room to be in the basement, but the captain led her up the stairs to a door on the second landing. "Visitor for you, Becket," he said and ushered Daisy into the room.

His manservant struggled up against the pillows. "Why, Daisy! You shouldn't be seeing me like this."

Harry retreated but left the door open. Becket's brown hair, which was normally neatly plastered down on his head above his thin white face, was sticking up all over his head. Daisy sat down beside the bed. "Has the doctor seen you?"

"Yes, but he says it's a feverish cold. I'll be right as rain in a few days."

"Captain does you proud," said Daisy, looking around the sunny room. The walls were lined with bookshelves. There was a leather armchair in front of the fireplace, and by the window, a handsome desk.

"Why did you come?" asked Becket.

Daisy told him about the captain's neglect and Rose's anger. "I think my master's really in love with her," said Becket, "and that's why he keeps clear of her because she can hurt him and he doesn't like being hurt."

"I think they love each other," said Daisy. "I think that's why she's so unhappy. She's treating me more like a servant than she's done in ages. But he said he'd take her to the ball tonight."

Becket sighed. "Let's just hope they see sense."

An hour later, Harry went to his office in Buckingham Palace Road. His secretary, Ailsa Bridge, was typing busily. The window behind her was wide open, but the air still smelt of peppermints. Harry believed his secretary was fond of peppermints, not realizing that Ailsa was fond of gin and drank peppermint cordial to disguise the smell.

"How are things?" he asked.

"Various cases have come in. The most immediate is from

Mrs. Barrington-Bruce. She will be wearing her diamonds tonight and fears jewel thieves and wants you to be on duty at her ball."

"I'll cancel that one. I'm escorting my fiancée and I do not think she would be pleased if I were there in the capacity of policeman. I will phone Mrs. Barrington-Bruce shortly." Harry went into his inner office and phoned Rose, only to be told that she was taking tea at Mrs. Barrington-Bruce's. He phoned Mrs. Barrington-Bruce's residence and asked the butler if he might speak to Lady Rose Summer.

Rose's heart gave a jolt when she heard his voice on the phone. "I just wanted to let you know that I shall be escorting you this evening," said Harry.

Her voice sounded cool and distant. "Alas, you are too late. I have already asked Sir Peter Petrey to escort me. How was I to know that you might remember at the last minute to honour our arrangement?"

"Look here—"

"Goodbye."

Harry glared at the phone. How dare she? He phoned again and this time asked for Mrs. Barrington-Bruce and said he would be there to guard her jewels.

Mrs. Barrington-Bruce was an indefatigable hostess. Because her entertainments were always lavish, she could attract the cream of society, people who would not normally take the trouble to travel as far as Kensington.

Daisy was becoming increasingly depressed. On the journey there, Rose had confided her worries about Dolly, saying that she thought the girl had some deep sorrow and was not just worried about the rules of society. Peter, an inveterate gossip, encouraged Rose to talk on and on about Dolly. Daisy was really beginning to fear that Rose was considering Peter as a marriage partner and furthermore she was jealous of Dolly. Somehow Daisy felt the class lines were so rigid that she could never be a real friend to Rose, whereas Dolly, who was acceptable in the eyes of society, had all the advantages.

Although hailed as a beauty, Rose, since her engagement, was no longer in such demand, and to her fury she had to sit out a whole three dances while watching her fiancé prowling around the place. She did not know he was working and assumed he was deliberately snubbing her. Her anger was so great that when Peter came up for his second dance she flirted outrageously, and the shrewd Peter, who knew exactly why she was doing it, played up to her.

Harry was furious. How dare she show him up like this? Mrs. Barrington-Bruce approached him. "I think you should dance with your fiancée," she said severely. "People do not know you are working for me and it looks as if you are deliberately cutting her dead."

He had not seen things from this angle but by the time he approached Rose, her flirtatious display on the dance floor had attracted many admirers and her dance card was full. He bowed instead before Daisy. "Miss Levine, will you do me the honour?"

Rose started to protest. "Miss Levine does not dance . . ." But her new partner had come to claim her and Harry was already leading Daisy onto the dance floor.

Daisy's little face, which still held a bit of her old pinched Cockney look, turned up to the captain's brooding one. "You asked for it," she whispered as they circulated in a waltz.

"I'm working," he hissed. "I'm supposed to be watching

Mrs. Barrington-Bruce at all times in case someone steals her jewels."

"But she's wearing 'em. Looks like a Christmas tree."

"Mrs. Barrington-Bruce fears some villain will rush across the ballroom and assault her."

"She's so corseted tonight in whalebone, it must be like armour," giggled Daisy. "But you are causing a lot of gossip, sir."

"I feel like asking Lady Rose to end this stupid farce of an engagement."

"You can't do that!" exclaimed Daisy. "She'll be shipped off to India and I'll have to go with her. Oh, do make a push to behave like a gentleman."

Her rather prominent green eyes were filled with worry. Harry gave a reluctant laugh. "I'll try."

But Rose's thoughts had been distracted from Harry. Dolly had slipped a note into her hand. Rose read it at the first opportunity. It said: "You are my only Frend. I am Running Away. Meet me at the Serpent at six tomorrow and I will tell *all*. Come Alone. Yr. Loveing Dolly."

"You're not really going, are you?" asked Peter on the road home. "Six o'clock! It's nearly two in the morning now."

"Dolly needs my help," said Rose firmly. "I will go."

"I'll come with you," said Daisy.

"No, she said to come alone and that's what I'm going to do. Ma won't miss me. She won't expect me to rise until one in the afternoon."

Rose let herself out of the family's town house at quarter to six in the morning and hurried in the direction of Hyde Park, unaware that Daisy was following her at a distance.

She assumed that Dolly would be waiting for her on the bridge over the Serpentine, where she had met her before. Rose shivered a little as she stood on the bridge. The weather had turned chilly. A duck squawked on the water below and Rose leaned on the bridge and looked over.

Then she let out a scream of fright, and Daisy, who had been hiding behind a nearby tree, scampered up to join her. Too upset to ask Daisy why she had followed her, Rose pointed downwards.

A rowing-boat was moored in the water by the bridge. In it lay Dolly dressed like the Lady of Shalott in the pre-Raphaelite illustration to Tennyson's famous poem by John Atkinson Grimshaw. Her filmy draperies floated out from the boat and trailed in the water. Flowers were woven in her hair. Her hands were crossed on her breast. Her beautiful face was clay-white.

"Is it a joke?" asked Daisy.

"No, look, there's blood on her dress."

Daisy looked wildly round the park. "Come away," she begged. "The murderer could still be hiding somewhere close."

"We must tell the police," said Rose.

And as if by some miracle she suddenly saw a policeman on his bike cycling through the park.

"Help!" screamed Rose. "Over here!"

Rose and Daisy clutched each other as the policeman cycled up.

"Miss Dolly Tremaine is down there," gasped Rose. "She's been murdered."

The policeman hurried down the river bank at the side of the bridge and bent over the body. Then he straightened up and came running back. He took out a notebook and wrote down their names. Then he said, "Wait here."

"Where's he gone?" whispered Daisy through white lips.

"There's a police box on Park Lane. It won't be long before he's back."

The gas-lit police boxes for use by the police and the public had started off in Glasgow a bare four years after the telephone had been invented. The cast-iron boxes looked like men's urinals.

They did not have to wait long. The policeman came back and began to take further notes. Who was the dead girl? Where did she live? Soon more police arrived and then two detectives, followed closely by Detective Superintendent Kerridge in a police motor car.

"Lady Rose!" he exclaimed, having dealt with two previous cases where Rose was involved. "What have you been up to now, my lady?"

TWO

‡‡

Gorgonised me from head to foot,
With a stony British stare.

—ALFRED, LORD TENNYSON

The earl's town house was in an uproar. Lady Rose and Daisy had been escorted home by Detective Superintendent Kerridge and Inspector Judd. The earl and countess were awakened to this dire news. They were told that the superintendent would return as soon as possible to interview Rose. What on earth had their daughter been up to now?

Kerridge had shrewdly guessed that he would be in deep trouble if he continued to interview Rose without her parents' being present. Unmarried girls were not expected to have any freedom at all. Their letters were routinely read by their parents before being handed to them. And they were certainly not expected to venture outside without being chaperoned. Kerridge was sure the earl would not consider Daisy to be a suitable chaperone without the added guard of a maid and two footmen.

Although it was noon before he arrived, having come straight from Dolly's parents, he had to wait some time until the earl and countess were dressed.

"You, again," was the earl's sour greeting. "What's our Rose been up to, then? It's those suffragettes, that's what it is."

"No, my lord," said Kerridge. "It is a case of murder."

"Where is my daughter?" shrieked Lady Polly.

"Here, Ma," said a calm voice from the doorway. Rose had gone to her rooms to get an hour's sleep.

"Who's murdered?" asked the earl. He tugged the bell-rope furiously and ordered a footman to fetch his secretary, Matthew Jarvis.

"A certain Miss Dolly Tremaine."

"Oh, that beautiful girl," wailed Lady Polly. "But what has all this to do with my daughter?"

Matthew came in at that moment and the earl roared, "Get Cathcart. He's got to come here now."

"Very good, my lord."

"Your daughter, Lady Rose Summer, had an appointment to meet Miss Tremaine at the Serpentine Bridge at six o'clock this morning."

"Why the deuce . . . ?"

"Miss Tremaine gave me a note at the ball last night," said Rose. "She said she was running away. When I arrived at the bridge, I looked over and saw her lying dead in that rowing-boat dressed as the Lady of Shalott."

"Who's she?" demanded the earl. "She ain't in Debrett's, I can tell you that. Foreigner, hey?"

"The Lady of Shalott is the title of a poem by Lord Tennyson, Pa. I have a copy of his poems here. This is the famous illustration, Mr. Kerridge."

"Any idea why she was dressed like that?"

"Miss Tremaine may have had the costume made to wear at a fancy dress ball next week."

"Have you any idea why she would want to run away?"

"I do not know. I only know that she was bewildered and unhappy in society. Her father is a country rector and her parents would expect her to marry someone with money to offset the cost of a Season."

"Nothing wrong with that," muttered the earl.

"I assume you have interviewed her parents," said Rose. "Have they any idea why she would want to run away?"

"None whatsoever," said Kerridge. "In fact, they say that she was about to be engaged before the Season even started. To a certain Lord Berrow."

"Lord Berrow is old," said Rose. "That is probably the reason she wanted to run away."

"Fiddlesticks," said Lady Polly. "The trouble is that girls these days will read cheap romances. One does not marry for love."

"Steady on, old girl," protested the earl.

"We were a rare exception," said Lady Polly. "Where is this rector's church?"

"Probably somewhere dire like Much-Slopping-in-the-Bog," said the earl. "Hey, rather neat that, what?"

Quite amazing, thought Kerridge. Their only child has just discovered a murder and yet they seem to have no concern for her welfare.

"Captain Cathcart," announced the butler.

"How did he get here so quickly?" asked the earl.

"He's got a motor car," said Rose.

"Nasty, smelly things. Never replace the horse. Sit down, Cathcart." The earl pointed a finger at Rose. "Rose is in trouble again."

Kerridge reflected briefly that one of his mother's lectures had been, "Don't point. Ladies and gentlemen don't point."

This lot would have been an eye-opener, thought Kerridge sourly.

"Lady Rose," he began, "discovered the murdered body of a Miss Dolly Tremaine early this morning." Harry listened intently as Kerridge outlined all he knew.

"What do her family say?" asked Harry. "Had she any enemies?"

"They are grief-stricken and bewildered. They do not know of any enemies."

"Any brothers or sisters?"

"One son, Jeremy, aged twenty-seven. I think they might come up with more information when they get over the shock."

"Odd, that," commented the earl. "Only two children. Thought those Church of England fellows bred like rabbits."

"Not in front of Rose," said Lady Polly. Then she stifled a sigh, thinking of all the little graves in the churchyard at Stacey Court, their country estate—all eight of Rose's little brothers and sisters who had died in childbirth.

"When did you leave the ball last night?" Harry asked Rose.

"Around two in the morning."

"And was Miss Tremaine still there?"

"I remember no longer seeing her around midnight."

"So sometime between, say, midnight and six in the morning, someone murdered her and dressed the body. You will need to search the rector's town house."

"The parents say her bed was not slept in. She planned to run away," said Kerridge. "She may have changed into that costume to please a lover who then murdered her."

"I don't like this," said Harry. "I think whoever murdered

her knew she was going to meet Lady Rose early in the morning. Lady Rose, do you still have that note?"

"I must have dropped it at the ball. But I remember putting it in my reticule, which I left with Daisy when I danced."

"We'd better have Daisy here."

Lady Polly ordered Daisy to be brought to the drawing-room.

When she entered, Kerridge said, "Lady Rose says she left her reticule with you while she danced. Did you leave it unattended at any time?"

"I left it on a chair when I danced with the captain," said Daisy. "I was sitting next to Countess Slerely. I usually do. Anyone picking it up and searching in it would be noticed."

"I think you danced with Captain Cathcart before Dolly gave me that note," said Rose. "Did you leave at any other time?"

"Well, one time I had to go to the you-know-what. That was just before midnight."

"I'd better call on Countess Slerely," said Kerridge. "Lady Rose, if you can think of anything else . . ."

"No, she can't," said the earl. "She shouldn't have been out at that ungodly hour unchaperoned."

"I was there," said Daisy.

The earl ignored her. "No more cycling for you, young lady. Go to your room."

"As for you," said the earl, glaring at Harry, "as my daughter is somehow involved in this, I expect you to clear things up as soon as possible. And while you're here, what do you think you are doing ignoring my daughter in such a manner?"

"I am sorry. My apologies, but pressure of work—"

"Pah! Behave yourself in future or I shall call off this ridiculous engagement myself."

"I wonder," said Harry later that day to his manservant, "where Dr. Tremaine got enough money to take a house for the Season and to furnish an expensive wardrobe for his daughter."

"He's well-connected," said Becket. "His aunt was Lady Tremaine and she married well and left him quite a large legacy."

"Where did you hear that?"

"You always tell me to listen to servants' gossip. The Running Footman where a lot of them drink is an amazing source of information."

"I suggest you take yourself there this evening and try to find out what you can about the family."

"May I have some money to entertain, sir?"

"Of course," said Harry, hurriedly pulling out his wallet. He drew out a large white five-pound note. "Will this be enough?"

"More than enough. I will bring you the change."

"You may keep any change for further bribery."

"Do you think, sir, that Lady Rose and Miss Levine will be safe?"

"Why?"

"The murderer may think that Miss Tremaine told Lady Rose much more than she actually did."

Harry shifted uneasily. "I am sure they will be all right. I wonder about Lord Berrow. He's in his fifties, is he not?"

"I believe so. He is a widower. Gossip says he drove his wife to an early grave with his womanizing."

"Indeed! So what was saintly Dr. Tremaine about to even consider handing his daughter over to such a man?"

"Lord Berrow is very rich."

"Ah. Do you not find our society very corrupt, Becket?"

"It is not for me to say. Will you be going out this evening?"

"Yes, I may as well call on my fiancée. Her father has accused me of neglect."

Harry had to wait quite a long time while the earl and countess argued over whether he should see their daughter. "I was hoping this deuced engagement would just fizzle out," said the earl.

"We should have sent Rose to India. Mrs. Fanshawe's daughter, who is mortally plain, went out and secured the affections of Colonel Brady. Nonetheless, perhaps if Rose sees more of Captain Cathcart, she will realize her folly. She does seem to be forming a tendre for Sir Peter."

And so they discussed and argued while Harry paced up and down the hall.

At last he was summoned and told that he might have fifteen minutes alone with Rose, provided the door of the drawing-room stayed open.

Before leaving them, Lady Polly watched as Harry rushed forward and, seizing Rose's hands in his, kissed them both. When she had gone, Rose, blushing, snatched her hands away and demanded, "What do you want?"

"I am concerned for your safety. As Becket has just pointed out to me, your life might be in danger. Do be very careful."

"I am tired of being careful," snapped Rose. "I am tired of dressing and undressing and sitting down to enormous banquets which might alleviate some of the misery of the poor of London."

"I thought you might be interested in finding out the identity of the murderer?"

Rose's blue eyes lit up with sudden interest.

"How could I do that?"

"This Lord Berrow. If I go to interview him, he will probably clam up. But if you were to meet him socially and start to talk about poor Dolly, then he might tell you more than he would tell either me or Kerridge."

In Scotland Yard, Kerridge was being told that his application to search the rector's town house had been refused and he also got a blistering lecture on his lack of sensitivity in proposing to add more grief to an already grieving family.

He felt tired. He had earlier interviewed Lord Berrow, who had simply stared insolently at him and then threatened to report him to the prime minister.

Harry heard a movement on the landing outside the drawing-room, gathered Rose in his arms and kissed her gently on the forehead just as Lady Polly entered the room.

"You may go now," said Lady Polly. "I have cancelled my daughter's social engagements for the next two days. After that, I will apprise you of her calendar and I expect you to be on hand to escort her."

"Delighted," said Harry and bowed his way out.

Outside, he could still somehow smell the light flower perfume that Rose wore and he swore so loudly that a lady walking her dog stared at him in outrage.

Two days later, Brum, the butler, brought in the morning post as usual on a small silver tray and placed it at the earl's elbow as his lordship was eating breakfast.

Rose looked at the little pile of letters. Had she been a man and not a girl, she thought angrily, any letters addressed to her would have been given to her unopened. Not that there was really anything personal addressed to her, but she lived in hope that perhaps Harry might write to let her know how the case was progressing.

The earl put down his knife and fork and riffled through the letters. Then he rang the bell. "Give these to Mr. Jarvis," he said to Brum. "Nothing of interest here."

"There is one letter addressed to Lady Rose," said Brum.

"Is there? I didn't notice. Let me have it."

"I really think I am capable of reading it myself," said Rose.

Her father paid no attention. He lifted up a letter and stared at it. Then he held out his hand and Brum handed him a letter opener from the tray.

"Harrumph, let me see. Good Gad!"

"What is it?" asked Lady Polly.

"Give me that letter, Pa!" shouted Rose.

"You go to your room, miss. You, too, Levine, and get Cathcart!"

"What can it be?" asked Rose, as she and Daisy sat in Rose's private sitting-room.

"Maybe one of your admirers sent an over-warm letter and Lord Hadfield's getting the captain to frighten him off."

Daisy stood up and walked to the mirror. Rose had presented her companion with a morning gown of white lace decorated with little red roses. Daisy admired her reflection in the glass and then wondered if she would ever have a chance to show it off to Becket.

She had an idea. "Maybe the captain will bring Becket with him and Becket will wait in the hall. I could nip down and see if he knows what's going on."

"Good idea. But you know what Pa is like. The captain will have simply been summoned without any explanation being given."

"I'll watch from the window and see if I can see them arriving."

Rose fidgeted while Daisy looked down from the window. At last, after what seemed like an age, she saw the captain's car stop outside, with Becket at the wheel.

"They're here!" cried Daisy. "Won't be long."

Daisy waited outside on the landing until she heard the captain being ushered into the breakfast room and then ran lightly down the stairs.

Becket was standing in the hall.

"Why, Daisy!" he exclaimed. "You do look like such a fine lady."

"Pretty, isn't it?" said Daisy, smoothing down her gown with complacent fingers. "What's going on?"

"At first the captain refused," said Becket in a low voice, "because he's busy and he doesn't like the way Lord Hadfield expects him to drop everything and come running. So the secretary, Mr. Jarvis, he phones back and says that Lady Rose has received a death threat."

"Oh, my stars and garters!" said Daisy. "This is bad. Rose has had a bad shock. She looks as cool as anything but I heard her crying during the night. I hope they don't decide to ship her off to India after all!"

"The story's been in all the papers. Probably some nutter."

"Probably a madman," Harry was saying. "I'll take this round to Scotland Yard. Kerridge will want to see if he can get any fingerprints off the letter. I mean, it must be from someone deranged." He studied the letter again. It consisted of letters cut out from magazines and the message read, "Dear Lady Rose, Keep your mouth shut about what Dolly told you or you'll be next. A Well-Wisher."

"I mean," Harry went on, "any sane person would assume that Lady Rose had already told Scotland Yard everything she knew."

Matthew Jarvis, standing behind the earl's chair, gave a slight cough. "If I may be so bold, my lord . . ."

"Go on. What is it?"

"There was an article in the *Daily Mail* yesterday which speculated that Lady Rose probably knew the dark secret of what had caused Miss Tremaine to say she was running away but was keeping quiet out of loyalty to her friend."

"Rubbish," said Harry. "Lady Rose barely knew the girl."

"How did the papers find out that my daughter was even involved?" raged the earl.

"I'm sure they have some pet policeman at Scotland Yard in their pay, not to mention the bribes they give to servants."

"A reporter tried to bribe me," said Brum. "But I sent him off with a flea in his ear, my lord. I told him I was due for a raise in salary anyway."

"Are you?" asked the earl, bewildered.

Harry looked briefly amused. "I think Brum means that he is now."

The earl twisted round and goggled at his butler. "Are you trying to blackmail me?"

The butler raised his gloved hands in horror. "I would not dream of it, my lord. But your lordship did promise me a raise in salary after a number of years."

"Did I? Oh, well, see to it Mr. Jarvis."

"My lord . . ." began Brum.

"What now?"

"If I may speak, my lord. It concerns Lady Rose and her dark secret."

"She doesn't have a dark secret!" howled the earl. "Oh, what is it?"

"The *Morning Bugle* has picked up on the *Daily Mail*'s story and has a large feature on Lady Rose about her involvement in previous murders and the fact that her fiancé is the captain here. They have published a photograph of Lady Rose taken a year ago at a garden party in which she looks sad. They say she must break the bounds of loyalty and tell the police what she knows. I did not wish to distress you, but several newspapers were on the doorstep yesterday."

Harry eyed Brum's impassive face and was suddenly sure that the butler had taken money from the reporters and had supplied them with fantasies about Rose in return.

"This is serious," said Harry. "I should have read the popular papers instead of the *Times*. I am afraid Lady Rose will need to be kept indoors until we are sure she is safe."

Rose was summoned. She turned slightly pale when she realized Harry was taking the threat seriously. Daisy had just told her about the letter.

"It may be just some crank," said Harry soothingly, "but it is as well to be safe."

Rose and Daisy were kept indoors. Rose had books to read to pass the time but Daisy felt she would die of boredom and repeatedly said she could not understand why the ban on going out of doors applied to her as well.

One bright sunny day after they had been kept in for almost two weeks, even Rose began to feel she could not bear this form of genteel imprisonment any more.

She stood by the window looking down at the square. "If only we could go outside for a little walk," she mourned.

"We could try," said Daisy eagerly. "Lord and Lady Hadfield have gone down to Stacey Court for the weekend."

"They might have told me. Why go into the country?"

"Some boundary dispute."

"I do think my parents are a trifle odd. They might have said something to me at dinner last night."

"Maybe they didn't want to tell you in case you thought it a good opportunity to get out of the house."

"Brum will stop us going. And what about Turner?" Turner was Lady Rose's recently hired lady's maid.

"I'll tell them you have a headache and want to be left alone," said Daisy eagerly. "Then we can wait until they are taking their luncheon and slip out. With my lord and lady being away, they'll be careless about guarding us. They'll be sitting down for luncheon any minute now. You wait here and I'll tell Turner to join the others for luncheon as she will not be needed for the rest of the day."

Rose waited eagerly for Daisy's return. Daisy was back after only a few minutes. "Let's wear our plainest clothes," said Daisy. "We don't want to attract any attention to ourselves, even though the press have given up watching the house."

They changed quickly, Rose into a straight skirt, striped blouse and jacket and sailor hat, and Daisy also into a blouse, skirt and jacket but with one of Rose's old straw hats embellished with flowers on her head.

They crept together down the stairs and quietly let themselves out through the front door and then scampered along the square, giggling and hanging on to each other, thrilled with the combination of sunshine and freedom.

"Where now?" panted Rose.

"Let's look at the shops and try on hats," said Daisy, happy that now she and Rose seemed to be friends again instead of mistress and companion.

By mid-afternoon, they realized they were hungry and went to the tea-room at Fortnum and Mason in Piccadilly.

William Fortnum, who founded the famous store, was a footman in the royal household of Queen Anne. His job was to replace the candles every night and he made a tidy profit out of selling the old ones. He also had a sideline as a grocer.

He persuaded his landlord, Hugh Mason, to go into the grocery business with him and Fortnum and Mason was born.

Daisy and Rose had salmon in aspic embellished with prawns and lobster before they got down to the serious cake-eating business.

They chatted happily about this and that and then began to discuss the threatening letter. "I am sure it was some crank," said Rose. "I am in no danger at all. I think we should sneak into the study and phone the captain. He must persuade Pa to let me go out again." She blushed suddenly, remembering again the feel of his lips against her forehead.

Rose paid the bill and they walked out into Piccadilly, knowing that they had to return home and beginning to feel depressed.

"Cheer up," said Daisy. "I'm sure it won't be long before

we're out and about." She stopped in front of a milliner's. "I say, do look at that hat. They must ha' slaughtered a whole aviary. It's got more stuffed birds on it than's decent."

"My lace has come untied," said Rose, stooping down.

There was a sharp report. The milliner's window shattered just as Daisy grabbed hold of Rose and fell back onto the pavement with her. People began screaming. Some man shouted, "He had a gun! He had a gun!"

Rose and Daisy got unsteadily to their feet. Daisy brushed shards of glass off their clothes with a trembling hand. Commotion surrounded them. The milliner came out screaming that they had broken her window. Others were saying someone had fired a shot. Finally, to Rose's relief, a constable pushed his way to the front, demanding to know what was going on.

"I d-don't know," said Rose, on the verge of tears.

"Someone tried to shoot her," said Daisy. "You should be asking for witnesses. He'll be miles away by now."

"You trying to tell me how to do my job, young lady? Let's be 'aving your name."

"I'm Miss Daisy Levine, companion to Lady Rose Summer. This is Lady Rose Summer."

More policemen arrived on the scene. Rose explained that as she bent down to tie her bootlace, a bullet had whizzed over her head and shattered the window. "I assume it was a bullet," she said, "because I heard someone shouting, 'He's got a gun.'"

A police inspector joined them just in time to hear Rose's last words. "Get into that crowd," he roared, "and get hold of anyone who saw this man."

At last a small, fussy elderly man was propelled through the crowd to the inspector.

"There was a lot of traffic, officer. I noticed him because he had an odd colour of red hair. He stood in the middle of the traffic behind a hackney carriage and I wondered why he did not cross. Then, as the traffic in front of him cleared, he pulled out a gun and fired."

"Age? What was he wearing?"

"He was wearing a long black cloak. Oh, and he had pince-nez. No hat."

Another two witness were brought forward. They said they had seen the man with the red hair and black cloak run away in the direction of the Green Park.

The inspector snapped out orders. The park was to be searched immediately and all the streets round about.

Kerridge had been talking to Harry when the phone on his desk rang. When he answered it, Harry, to his dismay, heard Kerridge exclaim, "Lady Rose! Shot! I'll be down there right away."

"Is she dead?" asked Harry. "Please don't tell me she's dead."

"No. Someone fired a shot at her in Piccadilly. She bent down to tie her bootlace and that's what saved her. Lady Rose is being escorted home. We'd better go there."

Lord and Lady Hadfield were heading back to London, a local policeman having been sent to tell them about the attack on their daughter.

"I've had enough," said the earl. "The only thing is to send her out of the country where she'll be safe. I must say Cathcart's been a fat lot of good at protecting her."

"It's Rose's fault," moaned the countess. "Always wilful. And what were the servants about to let her leave the house?"

"If Brum thinks he's getting any sort of raise in pay after this, he can forget it," raged her husband.

"I wouldn't do that," said Lady Polly uneasily. "He might talk to the press."

Rose was beginning to feel exhausted as she told her story over and over again to Harry and the superintendent. Matthew had told her that her parents were on their way back and she felt sure that nothing now would stop them from packing her off to India. Inspector Judd had been placed on guard outside the drawing-room to make sure none of the servants was listening outside the door.

"I think the fellow was probably wearing a wig," said Harry. "I mean the wig, the pince-nez and the black cloak are really all that anyone can remember. I think, Lady Rose, that it would be a good idea to get you out of London for a bit, but not to Stacey Court. You would not even be safe in your country home. I wish we could lock you up in a police station."

"Wait!" Kerridge held up a hand for silence. "I've got an idea."

Rose and Harry waited patiently while the superintendent sat lost in thought. He was a grey man with grey hair and bushy grey eyebrows. "I correspond still with a policeman in a village called Drifton, near Scarborough in Yorkshire. I met him once when I was up there on a case. Regular chap with a delightful family. Lovely village which no outsider visits. What if Lady Rose and Miss Levine here were billeted with him for a bit? He could do with a bit of extra money."

"I cannot see my parents' accepting that idea," said Rose stiffly. "Furthermore, I have no desire to live with a policeman in some Yorkshire village."

There was a commotion downstairs. The earl and countess had arrived home. They could hear the earl shouting, "Where is she? And get those damned reporters off my front step."

He entered the drawing-room, shrugging off his sealskin coat and dropping it to the floor. A footman picked it up and handed it to the earl's valet.

Kerridge thought it odd that Lady Polly did not hug her daughter. She simply sat down, unpinning her hat and handing it to her maid, before haranguing Rose for having dared to leave the house.

"I have an idea, my lady," said Kerridge. He told them about his policeman friend in the Yorkshire village.

The earl and countess stared at him in silence. Rose waited for her parents to tell the superintendent he was talking rubbish.

To her dismay, her mother said slowly, "How long would Lady Rose be away?"

"Several months, I'm afraid. Give us a chance to catch this fellow."

Rose's parents fell silent again. Lady Polly thought of months without having to worry and worry about her troublesome daughter. She and her husband enjoyed society but they had had little enjoyment recently because of fretting about Rose's odd engagement.

The earl was thinking that several months away from Cathcart and she might change her mind about this ridiculous engagement.

"Is this policeman respectable?" he asked.

"Oh, very," said Kerridge. "Good church-goer."

"And does he have children?"

"Got five young 'uns."

"Would the police station have enough room to house my daughter and Daisy?"

"Big old rabbit warren of a place. I'm sure he'd find room. I'll telephone him now, if you like."

"He has a telephone?" asked the earl, who thought that magic instrument was only confined to the upper reaches of society.

"Yes, he has, my lord."

"Why can't I stay with Aunt Dizzy in Scotland, or Aunt Matilda in Dover?" asked Rose.

"Because this murderer can find out who your relatives are and I don't want you anywhere where there are servants who might talk. Would you like me to telephone this man? He is P.C. Bert Shufflebottom."

Daisy giggled. "What a name!"

"I'll have you know, my girl, that Shufflebottom is a good old Yorkshire name."

The earl made up his mind. He rang the bell. "Get Mr. Jarvis here." When the secretary entered, he told him to take the superintendent to the telephone.

Rose hoped against hope that the policeman would refuse. How could she help Harry with the case if she was stuck up in the wilds of Yorkshire?

But Kerridge was soon back. "He says he'll be delighted. I assume, my lord, you will be paying him something towards their keep?"

"Yes, yes, Matthew will see to it."

"And," put in Harry, "I think Lady Rose and Miss Levine should only take a few plain clothes. They must also use public transport. I suggest a discreet police guard until they are on the train and I would suggest the night train to York. There is bound to be a connecting train to Scarborough in the morning. Where is the nearest station to Drifton?"

"A market town called Plomley."

"Right. They can get off at Plomley, and Kerridge will instruct this Shufflebottom to meet them there. None of the servants must know about this. Tell them they are leaving for Stacey Court. I think Mr. Jarvis can be trusted?"

"Yes," said the earl. "About the only one."

"Then he must look up timetables and make the arrangements. Shufflebottom must tell the locals that Lady Rose and Miss Levine are remote relatives from an until recently rich family now fallen on hard times."

"I do not want to go to Yorkshire," said Rose in a thin voice.

The earl rounded on her. "You'll do what you're told, my girl."

THREE

✠

The two divinest things this world has got,
A lovely woman in a rural spot.

—JAMES HENRY LEIGH HUNT

Despite her loudly proclaimed distaste at being sent off to live with a rural policeman, Rose began to feel a certain amount of excitement as they were smuggled out through the garden door of the town house and over a ladder placed on a wall at the back and so into the mews, where a closed carriage was waiting for them.

They were taken to Paddington Station to catch the midnight North Eastern Railway train to York. Because of the innovation of Pullman coaches in first class, there were now three classes: first, second and third.

Rose had been given first-class tickets to York but it had been suggested they travel second class to Plomley on the Scarborough line.

Daisy kept looking nervously over her shoulder, seeing assassins behind every station pillar. Smoke billowed out from the steam engines up to Brunel's high arched roof.

A porter loaded their luggage on board. No footmen had been allowed to accompany them. The servants would be told in the morning that Rose and Daisy had left during the night for Stacey Court.

They had the luxury of a sleeping compartment thanks to Mr. George Pullman's invention. When a Pullman car was attached to the funeral train carrying Abraham Lincoln's body, the demand for Pullman's product swiftly grew. Pullman died so hated by his employees in 1897 that his heirs feared his body would be stolen and so the coffin was covered in tar-paper and enclosed in the centre of a room-sized block of concrete, reinforced with railroad ties. Ambrose Bierce said, "It is clear the family in their bereavement was making sure the sonofabitch wasn't going to get up and come back."

Rose was beginning to feel that life might not be so bad after all. It was exciting to go to sleep over the chattering wheels. Only Daisy felt torn away from London, and the wheels sang a dirge on her ears: "Can't go back. Never go back. Can't go back." She peered out of the window and saw only her own reflection as the night-time countryside went flying past. The east coast line was in competition with the west coast line and the great steam engine could reach up to a hundred miles per hour. Daisy shuddered. They were flying into foreign territory. Yorkshire.

They tumbled out sleepily at York station at seven in the morning. They had arrived an hour earlier, but first-class passengers were allowed to stay on for breakfast.

Rose commanded a porter to take their luggage to the Scarborough train. Daisy followed behind, feeling once more like a servant, not knowing that Rose's autocratic behaviour was caused by her sudden nervousness. What if the would-be assassin had followed them onto the train and was biding his time?

In a fusty second-class compartment they were crowded by a large woman with four sleepy cross children who kept crying and wailing. Their mother seemed indifferent to their noise and distress.

Rose fretted and fidgeted, feeling the beginnings of a headache, and could only be glad when Daisy suddenly shouted, "Shut that bleedin' noise."

The children stared at her in awe and then mercifully fell silent.

The train stopped at station after station, until it finally drew into Plomley and settled down with a great hiss which sounded like a giant's sigh.

The mother prodded Daisy in the back with her umbrella as Daisy was leaving the compartment. "Just you wait till you got kids of yer own," she shouted.

Daisy whipped round. "If I had brats like yours, I'd drown them!"

Can't possibly be them, was P.C. Shufflebottom's first thought on hearing Daisy's remark. I was told to look for two grand ladies.

But then Rose descended and looked around. She saw the policeman in uniform and approached him.

"Mr. Shufflebottom?"

"Yes, indeed, ma'am. Good journey?"

"Yes, I thank you. As you probably know, I am Rose Summer and this is Miss Daisy Levine."

"Is that your luggage?" asked the policeman nervously, looking at a pile of suitcases and hat boxes.

"We decided to travel light so as not to occasion comment," said Rose.

Bert Shufflebottom signalled to an elderly porter. "Load the ladies' bags on the trap, Harry."

Rose thought briefly of that other Harry. Did he miss her? What was he doing?

The morning was cold, with patches of frost in the shadowy bits of the station platform.

They climbed into the trap outside the station. Bert made a clucking noise and the pony moved off.

"We don't have all that much room, ladies," said Bert. "I suggest you select the clothes you really need—we lead a simple life—and store the rest in the old stables at the back of the cottage."

"You do not live in the police station?" asked Rose.

"Got a tidy cottage next door."

"How old are your children?"

"Let me see, the eldest is Alfred—he's just finishing school this year. He's fifteen. Next is Lizzie, fourteen. Then there's Geraldine. Her's thirteen. After her comes Maisie at nine years. And then there's the baby, Frankie, nine months. Frankie was unexpected like, but we ain't complaining."

"We will do our best not to put Mrs. Shufflebottom to too much trouble."

"Oh, nothing bothers my Sally much. Looking forward to some grown-up female company, she is."

I'm not going to be able to bear this, thought Rose.

They fell silent until, after a few miles, Bert pointed with his whip and said, "That be Drifton, in t'valley."

Rose looked down the road to a huddle of houses crouched beside a river.

"And that's the river Drif. Get some good trout there. If Alfred's lucky with his rod arter school, we'll have trout for tea. I likes a nice bit o' trout."

Rose had expected Sally Shufflebottom to be an apple-cheeked countrywoman, but the woman waiting on the dirt road outside the cottage next to the police station was tall and thin with a severe mouth and grey hair scraped back into a bun.

She came forward to greet them. "I'm Sally," she said. "I've been instructed to call you just Rose and Daisy, not to occasion comment, like. My, my, look at all your luggage!"

"I told them to take out a few things and put the rest in the stables," said Bert. "T'won't do to look too fine and grand."

The cottage was a rabbit warren of small rooms. There was a kitchen-cum-living-room with a great black range along one wall on which two pots were simmering. It was furnished with a horsehair sofa, a long table flanked by upright chairs, and two armchairs on either side of the range. The floor was covered in shiny green linoleum with two hooked rugs.

"I'll show you your room," said Sally. She led the way along a stone-flagged passage and threw open a door. There was a double bed covered in a patchwork quilt, a dresser, a marble wash-stand holding a basin and ewer. A little table by the bed held a blue jug of wild flowers.

Daisy, used to poverty, realized that Sally had gone to a lot of trouble. The patchwork quilt was new and the room was clean and aired.

"Thank you," she said, while Rose stared around her as if visiting a prison cell. "We'll just sort out a few clothes and take the rest to the stables."

"I," said Rose haughtily, "would like a bath."

"Bath day isn't until Friday, when we fire up the copper in the wash-house," said Sally. The copper was a huge copper container with a fire underneath for washing the laundry.

Daisy threw a warning look at Rose. "I hear the river at the back of the house. We've got our swimming costumes. That'll do."

"I'll leave you to it. Dinner won't be long."

"Dinner?" echoed Rose faintly when Sally had left the room.

"They take dinner in the middle of the day." Daisy took out a bunch of keys and began to unlock their cases. "I'll get out our swimming costumes first."

The water in the river was so cold that they both plunged in and then scrambled out again and ran back into the house. Large coarse towels had been laid out on the bed. They scrubbed themselves down, Rose too cold to be ashamed of standing naked in front of Daisy.

They put on plain wool dresses and had just finished dressing when they heard Sally call, "Dinner!"

The Shufflebottom family were all seated around the table. The girls stared wide-eyed at Rose and Daisy.

"Sit down on those two chairs next to Bert," said Sally.

Dinner started, after Bert had said grace, with mutton broth followed by lamb stew and then apple crumble. Rose realized she was very hungry and had to admit the food was delicious.

Lizzie found courage to speak first. "Ma says you went swimming." She stared in awe at the elegant beauty that was Rose.

"One gets very dirty on a train," said Rose. "Your mother said bath day wasn't until Friday."

"You could have waited until then," said Lizzie. "Ma would have given you first water."

Maisie piped up. "By the time I get it, it's awful dirty."

Rose repressed a shudder and hoped the river would warm up soon.

"I'm sure you wouldn't mind us arranging our own baths," said Daisy, "if we find the wood and fire up the copper."

"If you're prepared to do that, lass," said Sally, "then I've no objections."

I must phone Captain Cathcart, thought Rose, and beg him to let us come back to London. "May I use the telephone in the police station?" she asked Bert.

"I'm sorry," he said. "Superintendent Kerridge said there were to be no further calls from here regarding yourself in case some girl on the exchange listens in."

When dinner was over and the children had left again for school, Sally told Rose and Daisy to go and lie down and take a rest.

"It's not too bad," said Daisy as she lay in the double bed next to Rose. "They're nice people."

"I shall go mad here," said Rose curtly. "Peasants do not amuse me."

"You rotten snob!"

Rose hunched over on her side. "I am going to sleep. I hope this will all turn out to be a bad dream."

"How do you think Lady Rose is doing?" Kerridge was asking Harry.

"Probably suffering and blaming me for everything. Lady Rose likes to be radical and think she's at one with the common people, just so long as she doesn't have to meet any of them."

"Then this visit will do her good. We're no further forward except for one little thing. Well, may not be a little thing."

"What's that?"

"The Honourable Cyril Banks proposed to Dolly and was turned down."

"Let me see, that one has a bad reputation from drinking and gambling. I feel sure Dolly's parents told her to turn him down. No money there."

"Anyway, I'm going to interview him."

"Mind if I come along?" asked Harry.

"Very well. But I'll get a lecture from Judd over allowing amateurs into a Scotland Yard investigation."

"What about the gun?"

"We got the bullet. It was embedded in some stupid hat covered in dead birds. Our expert thinks it came from a lady's purse revolver, maybe a 0.2500 French-Belgian one."

"Any gun of that type registered to anyone?"

"We're working on it. Let's go and see what the Honourable Cyril has to say for himself."

They tracked Cyril down to The Club in St. James's. His manservant had told them that was where he had gone. The gloomy Inspector Judd had at last to realize that there was some benefit in bringing Harry along, for The Club would not have allowed policemen, however high-ranking, past the entrance. Since Harry was a member, he was sent it to winkle Cyril out.

Kerridge waited outside until Cyril, protesting volubly that he would have Harry blackballed, emerged at last from The Club and was helped into the police car and they all drove to Scotland Yard.

In Kerridge's office, a flustered Cyril was still protesting. "It is disgraceful that I should be dragged out of my club like a common criminal. I shall report you to the Home Office."

"Settle down, Mr. Banks," said Kerridge. "Only a few questions and then you will be driven back to your club. Now, we believe you proposed marriage to Miss Tremaine and were turned down."

"So what?" said Cyril. He raised his monocle, screwed it firmly in one eye and glared at Kerridge.

"As you know, we are investigating her murder."

"Here, now!" exclaimed Cyril. "I'm leaving. You're trying to pin this murder on me!"

"Sit down, Mr. Banks. No one is accusing you of anything. We simply, at this stage, want to ask a few questions about Miss Tremaine. Did she say anything or give any indication that she was being threatened?"

"Well, no. In fact she prattled on about the countryside and how she missed it. Empty-headed sort of girl."

"If you thought her empty-headed, why did you want to marry her?"

Cyril looked at the superintendent as if he thought the man had lost his wits.

"She was the most beautiful girl I've ever seen. What did it matter whether she had a brain or not?"

"How did you take it when you were rejected by her?"

"*She* didn't reject me, the parents did. Never got as far as popping the question to her. I asked her father's permission and he told me she was meant for greater things. I told him she couldn't do better than me and who did he think he was anyway? A mere country rector. Silly little man."

"Did you threaten Miss Tremaine?"

"No, I danced with her after that and I said I wanted to marry her but her father wouldn't let me ask her and she burst into tears, right on the dance floor. Her mother came up and dragged her off. Disgraceful!"

Harry studied Cyril while the interview was going on. He could imagine such as Cyril being capable of murder. He was an extremely vain fop from the top of his bear-greased hair to his tiny patent leather boots. He had a smooth round barbered face, small eyes and a small mean mouth.

"Did she talk about any friends, any acquaintances?"

"No; may I go now?"

"I suggest you remain in London for the time being. If you have urgent business in the country, you must report to me."

"That's it!" said Cyril furiously. "I'm off. The Prime Minister shall hear of your treatment and no, I am not going back to The Club in your rotten motor car. I shall take a hack."

Rose awoke late the next day. There was no sign of Daisy. She washed and dressed and went through to the living-room.

"Where is Daisy?" asked Rose.

"She very kindly took the children to school and then said she would go for a walk. I'll make you some breakfast although they'll all soon be back for dinner."

Rose was feeling uneasy and ashamed of her remark about peasants. What if they had heard her?

Sally bent over her cooking pots. "It's Plomley Fair next week and the girls are crying out for new dresses, but I told them there isn't the money to buy new frocks every year."

Rose thought about all her gowns lying in suitcases in the stables. "I have a great deal of clothes I will not need while I am here," she said. "I will go out to the stables and select some items which can be made over for the girls."

Sally stared in amazement at the young lady she had thought was a chilly aristocrat. Rose suddenly smiled. "If I were to do something, the time would pass more quickly. That way it would please your little girls and it would please me."

"Well, in that case . . ."

"I'll go now," said Rose.

Daisy collected the children from school. She had already made a slingshot for Alfred out of a small forked branch and one of her garters and had bought sweets for the rest at the local village shop. "You're not to eat them, mind," she cautioned, "until after you've had your dinner."

She was still furious with Rose for being so high and mighty. Daisy was enjoying all this freedom of being away from the rigid class system of London's top ten thousand.

When they all crowded into the living-room, an amazing sight met their eyes. On the horsehair sofa were spread out gowns in fine muslins, silks and satins.

"Ah, Daisy," said Rose, "I was just saying to Sally that we could make over some of my gowns to provide the girls with new dresses for the fair."

The girls screamed with delight. "Silence," roared their father. "Say thank you to Miss Rose and sit down at the table."

"Do we have to wear our pinafores over them?" asked Geraldine.

"Of course," said her mother. "Girls of your age without pinafores? Won't do."

Bert said grace. The meal was faggots in a rich sauce, followed by rhubarb tart.

"We're going to be right fat by the time we leave here," said Daisy and everyone laughed.

Rose ate steadily, enjoying the food. The rich food she was used to had never spurred her appetite the way Sally's simple cooking did.

When Daisy went off to take the children back to school, Sally said, "I've a sewing-machine in the parlour."

The parlour was kept for high days and holidays. The sewing-machine was set up at a table by the window. The fireplace was stuffed with newspaper and the room was cold. A newer version of the horsehair sofa in the living-room dominated the parlour, along with two horsehair armchairs covered in slippery black leather. On the mantelpiece was a clock stuck forever at ten past twelve and on an occasional table sat a stuffed owl in a glass case. Against the wall opposite the window was an upright piano.

Sally saw her looking at it. "It's never played. Bert saved old Mrs. Carey's life once and she left him that in her will."

"I'm sure Daisy and myself can give your children lessons if you would like," said Rose.

Under her hard-looking exterior, Sally was actually shy and had been very nervous of housing this aristocrat and her companion. For the first time since they arrived, she began to feel at ease. "That would be lovely. I've got patterns there for all the girls. They had dresses made from them last year, but they've all grown a bit since then."

"I'll measure them all when they get home from school."

"Your beautiful gowns," said Sally awkwardly. "Won't you need 'em for yourself when you go back to Lunnon?"

"I can have more made," said Rose, giving Sally a glimpse of what is what like never to have to worry about money.

Mathew Jarvis was sending a very generous sum of money each week for Rose's and Daisy's upkeep. The thrifty Bert put it all in a savings account for his children's futures, keeping some back so that Sally could provide ample meals.

That evening, while Rose measured the girls and discussed which material they would like best, Daisy sat down at the piano and began to sing.

After finishing his beat, Bert was walking home with Dr. Linley, who lived farther along the road. The doctor stopped and said, "Listen!"

From the policeman's cottage came the sound of two voices. Rose had joined Daisy at the piano.

"You are my honeysuckle, I am the bee,
I'd like to sip the honey sweet
From those red lips, you see.
I love you dearly, dearly, and I
Want you to love me—
You are my honey, honeysuckle,
I am the bee."

"It's those girls, those distant relatives of ours," said Bert. "Seem to be settling in."

"Shh!" said the doctor.

Rose had started to sing "Just a Song at Twilight." Other villagers came to join them. The evening air was soft with a hint of summer to come.

Then a smart landau came along and stopped. "What's going on?" cried an authoritative voice.

"Lady Blenkinsop," muttered Bert gloomily. "We're listening to one of my relatives singing," he said aloud.

Lady Blenkinsop listened as well. "Very good," she said at last. "They will sing for me. Fetch them out."

What would Kerridge say to this development? wondered Bert. But Lady Blenkinsop, for all her airs and grand house, was only the widow of an ironmaster who had bought his title. And she never went to London.

The crowd waited until Rose and Daisy came out. There was a polite spattering of applause.

"Come here!" barked Lady Blenkinsop.

By the light of the carriage lamps, Rose saw a very small, sour-looking woman dressed in widow's weeds.

Daisy suddenly wished Rose would look, well, more *messy*. Even in a plain white blouse and skirt, Rose looked impeccable and she had dressed her hair fashionably.

Daisy curtsied but Rose held herself ramrod-stiff and demanded in glacial tones, "Yes?"

"Yes, what, my girl? I have a title."

"What do you want?" asked Rose.

"I want you and the other one to come and sing for me tomorrow afternoon."

"I am afraid we are otherwise engaged," said Rose. "Good evening to you. Come, Daisy."

Rose turned on her heel and strode back into the house.

"That uppity little minx needs a taste of the birch," fumed Lady Blenkinsop. "Drive on."

Two days later, Bert was summoned by the police commissioner in York. Lady Blenkinsop had accused him of insolence.

"I will go with you," said Rose.

"You'll make matters worse," groaned Bert.

Sally returned after seeing Bert off at the station. "Do not worry," said Rose. "If your husband is dismissed, then my father will support him."

The policeman's wife whipped round. "And you think that'll solve the problem, lass? My Bert's proud of his job. You've brought nothing but trouble."

———

"We must do something," whispered Daisy. "If only we could phone the captain."

"I could do that," said Rose. "I know we were told not to phone or write but I could pretend to be his cousin and talk in a sort of code. We must move quickly. We can't use the telephone in the police station or the girl in the exchange might tell Bert. I know, we'll get to Plomley. I'll just tell Sally we're going out for a walk. I do find all this use of first names rather peculiar, but Bert said it makes us sound more like family."

They hitched a lift to Plomley on a farm cart.

It was an old-fashioned wooden telephone kiosk in Plomley, not one of the new boxes.

Rose got through to the operator and gave her Harry's number, shovelled the required pennies into the slot and waited.

Let him be there, she silently prayed. Please let him be there.

Ailsa Bridge answered the phone. Rose asked to speak to the captain. "Who is calling?" asked Ailsa.

Rose thought quickly. "His cousin, Miss Shalott."

Harry came on the line. "This is your cousin, Miss Shalott," said Rose quickly. "Our uncle Bert is in trouble again, the old rip. The police commissioner in York has summoned him this morning. He must have been drunk and breaking windows again. Added to that, a certain Lady Blenkinsop has put in a complaint against poor old Uncle because she says I was rude to her and all because she wanted me to sing at her house, just like a common chorus girl. Too, too sickening. Do help Uncle Bert, please."

"Where are you telephoning from?"

"Such a quaint little wooden kiosk. You know Mama will

not let me use the telephone and she says that Uncle Bert should be left to his own devices."

"I'll deal with it right away. Are you well?"

"Oh, yes, very well. Thank you."

Rose replaced the receiver. "Let's hope he gets to the commissioner in York in time, Daisy."

Bert stared miserably at his shiny regulation boots as he sat outside the commissioner's office. He would do anything to avoid losing his job. But Kerridge had sworn him to secrecy.

At last a police officer emerged from the commissioner's office and said, "Go in now."

Bert, with his helmet tucked underneath his arm, went in.

The commissioner, Sir Henry Taylor, was a bluff, red-faced man. "Sit down, Shufflebottom," he said. "You must be thirsty after your journey. Tea?"

Bert blinked in surprise, too startled to speak.

"I know, you'd probably like a beer. Tretty," he said to the attendant police officer, "fetch Mr. Shufflebottom a beer and bring me one as well. Now, there's been this complaint from Lady Blenkinsop."

"I—I'm right sorry," stuttered Bert. "You see, sir, what happened—"

"Never mind. That old witch is always complaining about something. Ah, beer, just the thing. Drink up."

"Your health, sir." Bert raised the tankard with a shaking hand.

"I've been looking at your record. Very fine. No scandals. Everything dealt with quietly and decently. Then you rescued that family last year in Plomley at the fair when their carriage horse bolted. The reason I called you in was to tell you that we think the time has come to give you a little rise in salary as a token of our appreciation."

"Oh, sir, thank you, sir. What about Lady Blenkinsop?"

"The lord lieutenant is calling on her. You will not be troubled by her."

Lady Blenkinsop was initially delighted when the lord lieutenant, Sir Percy Twisletone, called on her. She longed to mingle with the aristocracy, but they mostly shunned her.

"I will get right to the point," said Sir Percy. "You have put in a complaint against the village policeman because of his relative's behaviour."

"Of course! Cheeky minx. I honoured her with an invitation to sing for me and she refused!"

"Miss Rose comes from a very distant aristocratic branch of the family, fallen on hard times."

"I find it hard to believe that Shufflebottom has any aristocratic connections."

"They may have been, shall we say, on the wrong side of the blanket, but royalty—excuse me, I should not have said that—certain sins must be forgiven."

Lady Blenkinsop goggled at him. "Do you mean . . . ?"

"I said nothing," said Sir Percy sternly. "I only came to warn you to be careful whom you insult in future. The news can travel upwards to amazingly high circles."

"Oh, dear," babbled Lady Blenkinsop. "I shall apologize."

"No, you will not say anything of this matter and you will not go near the policeman again. We have eyes and ears everywhere and if you tell anyone about this, I shall find out."

Sally collected the children from school herself. She could hardly bear to speak to either Rose or Daisy. She drove the children to Plomley Station in the pony and trap. They all held hands as they saw the train rounding the curve. Sally stood holding baby Frankie in her arms. We'll get through this together, she thought.

She stared in amazement as Bert descended from the train with a bunch of roses in one hand. His smile was so wide it seemed to split his face in half.

She ran to meet him and Frankie set up a wail at being jogged about on her hip.

Bert bowed and handed her the roses. "I've got a raise," he said. He fished in his pocket and brought out a paper bag of aniseed balls and handed them round. "We'll even be able to go to Scarborough this year for a holiday."

Sally began to cry with relief. When she could speak, she asked, "What about Lady Blenkinsop?"

"The lord lieutenant's dealing with her. This is Rose's doing. I know it is. She didn't use the phone, did she?"

"No, but Dr. Linley said that he saw them on Farmer Jones's cart heading towards Plomley today and then they came back in a hired carriage."

Rose was sewing at the machine in the parlour when they came in and she smiled with relief when she saw all the happy faces.

"Everything all right?" she asked.

Sally rushed forward and hugged her. "I don't know how

you did it, but Bert's got a raise and Lady Blenkinsop won't be troubling us. I'll get tea on."

The children were so excited about their new frocks and about going to the fair that Rose decided to dress up for the occasion, never thinking for a moment that by doing so she was putting her life at risk.

Rose had given Sally one of her best hats, a leghorn straw embellished with little yellow silk flowers.

"You do look a picture," said Bert to his wife, his face beaming with love. Rose felt a pang. This policeman saw his thin, hard-faced wife as beautiful. That was real love. Would any man ever look at her like that?

The day of the fair dawned sunny and warm. Rose was wearing a white lace gown embroidered with blue forget-me-nots. On her head she wore a straw hat covered in silk forget-me-nots. A fine cashmere shawl was thrown round her shoulders and she carried a white lace parasol. Daisy was wearing a green silk gown with a little rakish green hat perched on her curled hair.

The fair lasted two weeks. They decided to visit on the second week, after the horse fair was over, because the gypsies raced each other up and down the main street and there were always accidents.

They wandered around the dozens of stalls. The children clamoured for brandy snaps filled with cream and then walked around to look at the gypsy caravans where the women sat outside making pretty little pincushions stuffed with bran to sell at the fair.

Bert was on duty, so Sally kept near him, pushing the baby in a pram made out of an orange box and an old set of wheels.

The children dragged Rose and Daisy to the steam round-abouts and Rose good-naturedly helped Daisy lift the smallest child up onto the brightly painted horses before climbing on herself. How wonderful it was to ride round and round while the barrel organ churned out music-hall songs. The current favourite was: "Oh! Oh! Antonio, he's gone away—left me on my own e-o, all on my own e-o, I'd like to meet him and his new sweetheart, then up will go Antonio—and his ice cream cart."

Dr. Linley stopped to watch them. He was a keen amateur photographer. He raised his new Kodak camera just as the carousel slowed to a halt and snapped a photograph of Rose sitting side-saddle on the painted horse.

In the evening, he developed the photographs in his darkroom. He stared at the photograph of Rose. It was perfect. She was holding on to her hat and her lips were curved in a smile.

There was a new magazine for amateur photographers and they offered a prize every year for the best photograph. The next day, Dr. Linley entitled the photograph "A Summer's Day at the Fair," and posted it off.

The year moved into high summer, and in July Bert took two weeks' leave and they all went on holiday to Scarborough on the Yorkshire coast.

Daisy reflected that she had never seen Rose so happy. She took the children swimming and never once did she complain about the rather seedy lodging-house where they stayed.

Sally's face was filling out now that, thanks to the payment from Rose's family, they could afford good food at every meal, and she was not so careworn looking after the children, as Rose and Daisy took the burden of that duty off her hands. For the first time in years, she and Bert were able to spend time alone together.

When they returned to the village they were all glowing with good health. Rose started to organize a concert to raise funds to repair the school roof. Daisy was to be the star performer, but Rose had promised to sing one song.

The village hall was packed when Rose, accompanied by Daisy, walked onto the stage and began to sing:

> *"Birds in the garden, all day long, singing for me their happy song*
> *Flowers in the sunshine, wind and dew, all of them speak to me of you;*
> *You that I long for, near or far, you that I follow, like a star,*
> *Day may be weary, weary and long, you will come home at evensong.*
> *When you come home, dear, all will be fair,*
> *Home is not home if you are not there;*
> *You in my heart, dear, you at my side,*
> *When you come home at eventide."*

Rose sang with a depth of feeling Daisy had never heard in her voice before. She thought of Becket and wondered whether Rose had been thinking of the captain.

There was a great roar of applause.

Rose took Daisy's hand and led her forward. Then they both bowed, and just as they bowed, a shot rang out.

Women screamed, Bert blew his whistle, Daisy dragged a trembling Rose from the stage. "He's here! He's found us," whispered Rose.

FOUR

✝✝

Why should your fellowship a trouble be,
Since man's chief pleasure is society?

—SIR JOHN DAVIES

Two days had passed since the attempted murder of Lady Rose Summer. The countryside round about had been scoured for the would-be assassin. All railway stations were watched. Bert had a description of the man. He had called in at the village pub, The Feathers, with a magazine and had shown a photograph in it to the landlord. The photograph had won the annual prize and the story with it said it had been taken by a Dr. Linley of Drifton in Yorkshire.

"I didn't know any better," protested the landlord. "You didn't say to tell no one about her. I told him, 'Oh, that's Rose what lives with our policeman.'"

He described the man as being of medium height, stockily built, with a large red face, a brown moustache and wearing a dark suit and a bowler hat.

Kerridge had travelled to the village accompanied by Harry and Inspector Judd. Rose and Daisy were confined to the cottage and told not to venture out of doors.

Kerridge said to Bert, "It's no use you fretting, Shuffle-bottom. It's not your fault. How were we to guess that wretched doctor would take a photograph of her? From the description, it's no one we know. The Honourable Cyril isn't at all like the description of this stranger in the village."

"What about Dolly's brother, Jeremy?" asked Harry.

Kerridge shook his head. "No, Jeremy Tremaine is thin and tall. What are you getting at? That her own family would kill her? Rubbish."

"It did cross my mind," said Harry. "They were so blatantly ambitious."

"What I can't understand," said Kerridge, "is why he's still after Lady Rose? As I said before, he must surely know that she would have told the police everything."

"Cyril could have hired someone," said Harry. "I mean, he might blame Rose for his rejection."

"But she knew Dolly only for a very short time."

"He might not know that. There was also that speculation in the newspapers that Lady Rose might be keeping quiet out of loyalty to her friend. How did he manage to escape from a hall full of people?"

"He stood by the side door and fired and then escaped out into the night. Everyone was screaming and tumbling about, trying to escape. Lots of confusion. No one really saw him because they were all looking at Lady Rose and Miss Levine on the stage. Lady Rose can't continue to stay here. What are we to do with her?"

"Her parents are in Biarritz. You managed to keep this out of the newspapers?"

"Yes, clamped down on the whole thing."

"I see no reason to tell them of this." Or poor Lady Rose

really will be shipped out to India, he thought, "With any luck we will have solved the case by the time they return. I suggest Lady Rose should return to London. My Aunt Phyllis will act as chaperone and I myself will move into the earl's town house."

"If you gentlemen would like to discuss this over dinner," said Bert. "My Sally's just fed the children and they've gone back to school. Lady Rose will take dinner with you and you can tell her your plans."

Harry was taken aback to find Rose standing over the cooking pots on the range, wrapped in a long white pinafore. Daisy was laying the table with the help of Sally.

Rose turned round as they entered. "Please sit down," she said. "I am about to serve."

She lifted a leg of lamb out of one oven and then a tray of roasted potatoes and vegetables out of the other. She put the potatoes and vegetables in a casserole and placed it on the table and then put the leg of lamb on a large dish and put it in front of Harry. "Will you carve, please? I do not have the skill."

I will never understand the upper classes, thought Kerridge. Here is the captain, her fiancé, and yet she goes on as if he's a stranger.

When they were all seated over plates of lamb, Rose asked, "How are your investigations progressing?"

"Not well at all," said Kerridge. "By Jove, this lamb's delicious. You will make the captain a good wife. How are you coping with the shock, Lady Rose?"

"I am managing," said Rose stiffly, remembering how, last night, she had clung on to Sally and wept.

"We have decided that you should return to London," said Kerridge. "We saw no reason to alarm your parents with news of this. The captain's Aunt Phyllis will chaperone you and the captain himself will move into the town house as well."

Daisy brightened. Living with the captain meant living with Becket.

"May Daisy and I not stay here?" asked Rose. "He will surely not try to come here again and it is easier to watch out for strangers in a small village than it is in London."

"There's miles of places around this village where he could lie in wait," said Kerridge. "I will arrange for you to make a press statement saying that you only knew Miss Tremaine briefly and she never said anything about anyone. There was only that note about her running away."

"Lady Rose's photograph was in the newspapers after the death of Dolly Tremaine," said Harry. "Maybe one of the locals recognized her and blabbed."

"If one of the locals had recognized her and it had got about, the press would have been here," said Kerridge. "No, it was that doctor's photograph that did the damage. May I have some more lamb?"

Rose felt tearful the next day as she said goodbye to Sally, Bert and the children. Harry, waiting beside the closed carriage that was to take them to York, saw the way her lip trembled and was amazed that the usually haughty Lady Rose had formed such an affection for these people.

"I shall come back, I promise," said Rose, hugging Sally.

The children began to cry. Daisy cried as well, although,

unlike Rose, she was longing to get to London again and see Becket.

Rose was silent on the long journey. Harry made several attempts to engage her in conversation, but she only answered in dreary monosyllables.

But as the train from York was approaching Paddington, Rose suddenly asked him, "What is this aunt of yours like? Who is she?"

"She is Lady Phyllis Derwent, widow of Lord Derwent. She is very kind."

"It is nearly August," remarked Rose. "Lady Phyllis will not be obliged to do very much chaperoning. Everyone goes to Scotland in August to shoot things."

"Then you will have time to rest after your horrible experience."

Aunt Phyllis was waiting for them. Her butler answered the door to them, Brum having gone to Biarritz with the earl and countess. Unlike Brum, the butler, Dobson, was a small round genial man with mutton-chop whiskers and small twinkling eyes.

They followed him up to the drawing-room. Aunt Phyllis rose to meet them. She was a thin, languid lady, dressed in a sea-green tea-gown bedecked with many long necklaces of pearls mixed with arty lumps of decorated china beads strung with black thread. Her long face was highly painted. Her eyes were a pale washed-out blue under wrinkled lids. The hand she extended to Rose was covered in rings.

"Welcome," she said. "I trust you had a good journey?"

"Yes, I thank you."

"Such a too, too sickening experience. I do not know what Harry was about, to billet you with the peasantry."

"They were not peasants." Rose fixed her with a hard stare. "In fact they were decent charming people with no false airs or graces. I was happy there."

"Dear me. How original." Aunt Phyllis turned to Harry. "Is Rose to be kept indoors?"

"No, through Superintendent Kerridge a statement is being issued to the press today to say that she knew very little about Dolly Tremaine."

Becket entered the room and Daisy wished she could throw herself into his arms.

"Ah, Becket," said Harry. "Any news?"

"The Tremaine family departed for their home in the country some time ago. The son, Jeremy, is studying divinity at Oxford."

"I would really like to talk to the Tremaines now that their grief will have subsided a bit. Where do they live?"

"Dr. Tremaine is rector of Saint Paul's in the village of Apton Magna in Gloucestershire."

"I will go with you," said Rose.

"That will not do at all," said Aunt Phyllis. "I forbid it."

"You are a guest in my home," said Rose coldly, "so may I point out you are not in a position to forbid anything."

"My sweet child! Do not be in such a taking. I was merely concerned for your welfare," said Phyllis. She did not want to give up free accommodation and free meals for herself and her servants.

"As it is better I should be with my fiancée every time she ventures out of doors," said Harry, "then perhaps it would be a good idea if she accompanied me."

Lord and Lady Hadfield were basking in the sun on the terrace of the Grand Hotel at Biarritz. The earl was asleep with a newspaper over his face.

His wife poked him awake with the point of her parasol.

"Brum says you received a telegraph this morning. What was it?"

"Hey, what? Oh, that? Simply Cathcart saying that all was well with Rose."

"Such a relief," sighed Lady Polly, looking out at an expanse of deep blue sea. "It is so pleasant to be spared the worry of her."

"I wish I had a son," complained the earl. "Boys are less trouble."

"Oh, go back to sleep," snapped his wife, thinking again of all those little graves in the churchyard at Stacey Court. It wasn't as if she hadn't tried and tried. She had given birth to three boys, all of whom had died in childbirth and had gone to join their little sisters in the family grave. Only Rose had survived. Difficult Rose.

To Daisy's dismay, the captain had changed his mind about staying at the earl's town house. He had decided that it might occasion too much unfavourable comment, given that he was only engaged to Rose and not married to her.

But at least she and Becket were to join Rose and Harry on the outing to Gloucestershire.

Both wearing carriage dresses and heavily veiled, they climbed into Harry's car the following day.

The sun was shining and the shops and houses of London

all had blinds and awnings, fluttering in the lightest of breezes. They gave the effect of a city under full sail.

Harry was driving with Rose beside him. Rose was over-awed by the beauty of the motor car. It was the new Rolls-Royce Silver Ghost, the genius of the odd alliance between Charles Rolls, an aristocrat, and Frederick Royce, a working man from very poor beginnings. The Silver Ghost cruised along beautifully, keeping to the speed limit of twenty miles per hour.

"Your business must be doing very well," she remarked.

"Because of my Rolls?"

"Yes."

"Business has been excellent if tiresome. But people are pre-pared to pay a fortune for me to cover up scandals or even to find their lost dogs. I have told my secretary, however, that I am not taking on any further business until this case is solved."

They stopped at an inn in a village outside Oxford for lunch because they had set out early that morning. "I wonder if Jeremy Tremaine is at the university," said Harry.

"Hardly." Rose poked at the food on her plate. She would not confess that she was still nervous and frightened, expect-ing assassins to jump out from behind every bush. "It's high summer. What college does he attend?"

"Saint Edwin's."

"I wonder if this visit to the Tremaines is really necessary. They cannot know anything and they will hardly admit they drove their daughter into trying to run away because they were forcing her into marriage with Lord Berrow."

"They might just know something," said Harry. "If you've finished toying with your food, we'll get on the road again."

Inspector Judd entered Kerridge's office looking excited. "A man's been dragged out of the Thames under Westminster Bridge."

"So?"

"He hadn't been in the water long and he looks like the man from Plomley." The police artist had made a sketch of Rose's would-be assassin from the Plomley landlord's description, and the picture, prominently displayed on posters, had already been distributed to every police station in Britain.

Kerridge leaped to his feet and grabbed his bowler hat. "We'd best get down there and have a look."

The body was lying, covered with a blanket, on the landing stage at Charing Cross. "Anything in his pockets?" asked Kerridge.

"I recognized him from the poster," said the policeman, "and left him just as he was when he was dragged out of the river and gave instructions that you should be informed, sir."

"Good lad. Let's have a look."

The constable pulled back the blanket. "He can't have been in the water long," commented Kerridge. "Who found him? Where exactly was he found?"

"It was low tide and two children found him, half in, half out of the river."

"That artist did a good job. Let's see what he has in his pockets."

Kerridge knelt beside the body and began to pull out the contents of the dead man's pockets. There was a gold watch, a wallet containing a wad of notes, a blackjack, and, in one coat pocket, to Kerridge's delight, a pistol—a lady's purse pistol. "This looks like our man," said Kerridge. He turned the body over with the help of Judd. Someone had struck the man a vicious blow on the back of the head.

Kerridge sat back on his heels. "I think that's what killed him, not drowning, but the pathologist will let us know. Let me have a proper look in this wallet."

He carefully extracted the sodden notes, all five-pound ones. "I think there's about five hundred pounds here," he exclaimed. "Anything else?"

He fished out a photograph showing the dead man posing on a beach with a pretty woman. "I want the police photographer to make copies of this and send it to all the newspapers. Where is he, anyway?"

"Here, sir," panted the photographer, running up. Kerridge heaved the body back over. "Take a photograph of this, and take this photograph I found in the man's wallet and see if you can photograph it and send it round to the newspapers. When we know who he is, we'll know why."

Before reaching Apton Magna, they had driven through some very pretty villages, but Apton Magna seemed a dreary, poverty-stricken place. It consisted of a long line of agricultural labourers' cottages, built like miners' cottages, directly onto the road and without front gardens. At one end of the row was a village shop and a pub, which was just really someone's house with a green branch outside to show it sold ale. At the other end was the church with its square Norman tower.

The rectory was, however, a large handsome Georgian building with a porticoed entrance.

Dr. Tremaine came out to meet them. He was as thin as his wife was fat, wearing black clericals and buckled shoes. He had a craggy lantern-jawed face and small hazel eyes which regarded them with alarm.

"What are you doing here?" he demanded as Harry stepped down from the car.

"Lady Rose was fond of your daughter and wondered whether on calmer reflection Miss Tremaine had said anything to indicate there was anyone she feared."

"There was no one. Now, go away."

"Dr. Tremaine, I fail to understand your attitude. You must surely want to know who killed your daughter."

"That is a job for the police and not for some dilettante aristocrat like you."

"At attempt has been made twice on the life of my fiancée, Lady Rose," said Harry sternly, "and all because some madman thinks she may have some knowledge of the murderer, which, believe me, she most certainly has not."

"You must respect our grief," said Dr. Tremaine. "You must go away before my wife sees you. She is still gravely upset and her nerves are delicate."

At that moment, Mrs. Tremaine lumbered out of the house. With a cap on her mousy hair and her round figure, she looked rather like the late Queen. "Why, Lady Rose!" she exclaimed. "How kind of you to call."

"They're just leaving," snarled her husband.

"Oh, you cannot go without taking some refreshment. Don't be such a bear, dear. Do come in, Lady Rose."

Under the rector's glaring eyes, Rose entered the house. Daisy and Becket would have followed, but Mrs. Tremaine looked at them in horror. "Your servants may remain in the car."

She led the way to a drawing-room. It had noble proportions which were lost in over-furnishing. The light was dim because of three sets of curtains on the long windows—net, linen and then brocade.

Mrs. Tremaine pulled the bell-rope and when the maid answered the summons asked for tea to be brought in. "My poor Dolly was so honoured by your friendship, Lady Rose," she said. "She was meant for great things and struck down in her prime."

"Have you any idea who might have murdered her?" asked Harry.

"I have already answered that," said Dr. Tremaine.

"There was one person," said Mrs. Tremaine, dabbing at her eyes with a lace handkerchief, although Rose noticed her eyes were quite dry.

"Who?" asked Rose eagerly.

"The Honourable Cyril Banks, that's who. He asked Mr. Tremaine for permission to pay his addresses and was told the answer was firmly no. 'You'll regret this,' he shouted. 'I'll ruin that girl of yours. I'll get even with you.' Ah, here is tea."

Ludicrously, Mrs. Tremaine began to brag about the great people she had met in London, and about what a duchess had said to her and what a countess had confided in her, and Rose could practically hear all these dropped names pattering like rain among the china cups.

She played her part, flattering Mrs. Tremaine and listening intently to her. Then, as they rose to take their leave, Rose said, "May I perhaps see my old friend's bedchamber? An odd request, but it would help me to say goodbye."

The rector muttered, "Pah!" But Mrs. Tremaine could not refuse a title anything. "Follow me, my lady."

Upstairs, Rose stood on the threshold of what had been Dolly's bedchamber and looked in. It was a bleak room furnished with a narrow bed, a desk, a hard chair and a wardrobe. Above the fireplace was a badly executed oil painting of a blond and blue-eyed Jesus suffering a group of remarkably

British-looking children to come unto Him. The only other piece of furniture was a bedside table with a large Bible placed on top of it.

"Miss Tremaine did not have a diary or anything like that?" she asked.

"No, nothing like that."

"Thank you," said Rose.

"May I visit you when I am in London?" asked Mrs. Tremaine eagerly.

"By all means," said Rose, confident that the rector would make sure his wife would not.

Rose and Harry told Daisy and Becket the little they had learned. "Perhaps when everyone returns to London, I might encourage the attentions of Cyril and see what I can find out," suggested Rose.

"You are engaged to me," snapped Harry. "It would be regarded as most unseemly behaviour."

"Pooh," said Rose. Daisy and Becket exchanged looks. Their hopes of Rose and Harry's marrying seemed farther away than ever.

Harry received a message from Kerridge the following morning, bringing him up to date on the latest development.

He rushed round to Scotland Yard.

"Who is he?" he demanded, after entering Kerridge's office. All the way to Scotland Yard he had been praying that it would turn out to be someone Dolly had known, that the murderer had drowned himself in a fit of remorse, and that Rose would now be safe.

"Sit down," said Kerridge. "I've just interviewed a retired prison officer from Wormwood Scrubs. He says he recognized our man from his photograph in the newspapers this morning. His name is Reg Bolton. He was doing time for stealing a reticule up the West End from a lady who had left it lying beside her on a chair in a coffee shop. He had a record of violence as well. His wife was found dead with her head bashed in but this Reg had various people to alibi him for the night she was killed, so he got off with that one. Reg had five hundred pounds in his wallet when we found him. And no, he didn't drown. He was murdered."

Harry sat down in the chair opposite Kerridge. "So it looks as if someone hired him to kill Lady Rose?"

"That's just the way it looks to me," said Kerridge gloomily. "This gets worse and worse. He had a lady's purse pistol on him. I'm sure it'll turn out to be the one that was used. Blast!

"Did this Reg have any visitors when he was in prison?"

"Wasn't allowed any. If his wife had still been alive or if he'd had any children, then the authorities would have allowed them to visit, but no one else got in."

"May I talk to this screw myself?" In Pentonville Prison in 1840, prisoners were supposed to turn a crank on a machine. If the prisoner was to be punished further, the screw was tightened, and so that was how prison warders came to be known as screws.

"I'll give you a note. His name is Henry Barker."

Giving Becket the rare treat of taking the wheel of his new motor, Harry went to Wormwood Scrubs. He saw the governor and gave him Kerridge's note and Henry Barker was summoned.

"I have Detective Superintendent Kerridge's permission to interview you," said Harry. "I am Captain Cathcart."

"I've heard about you," said Barker. "Private detective, in't you?"

"That is correct. Now what sort of character was this Reg Bolton?"

"Brutal. He terrified a lot of the prisoners."

"Did he say anything to you, anything that might give us a hint that someone might be paying him?"

"Well, these hardened criminals always like to brag, Captain. The day afore he was leaving, he was grinning all over his face.

"'One more day to go,' I says. He says, 'I ain't coming back ere no more,' he says. 'Good,' says I. 'Mending your ways?' He grins and says to me, 'I'm going to be a gent. I got connections. Got a good job waiting for me.'"

"And what did you gather from that?"

"Villains never change. I thought maybe one of the other villains had put him in touch with a gang."

"Did he have a particular friend?"

The warder shook his head. "The others detested him, even the real hard ones. He was a nasty bit of work. I mean, I'm only guessing one of them offered him a job. But I never saw him talking much to anyone all the time he was here."

"How long he in here for?"

"Two years."

"And no one visited him during all that time?"

"No, sir. Not a one."

Harry turned to the governor. "Would it be possible to find me his home address?"

"I'll get my secretary to look up the records," said the governor. "Thank you, Barker, that will be all."

Harry left and headed for Bermondsey and to the address the governor had given him. He changed his mind when he saw the attention his Rolls was getting from bunches of sinister-looking men on street corners. "Turn around, Becket," he ordered. "We'll leave the car somewhere safe and take a hansom."

They returned later, told the cabbie to wait, and stared up at a rat warren of a building.

They entered a narrow hallway, edging around broken prams and soggy boxes of detritus. There was no reply on the ground floor and so they mounted the rickety stairs. The smell was appalling. Harry knocked at a door on the first landing.

A slattern of a woman answered it.

"I wondered if there was anyone living here who remembers Reg Bolton?"

"Never 'eard o' 'im." The door began to close.

Harry put his foot in it. "Is there anyone who has been living here for some time?"

"Try old Phil at the top and get your bleedin' foot out o my door."

Holding his handkerchief to his nose, Harry, followed by Becket, went on up the stairs. He knocked on one door and there was no answer. He tried the other one. There came the sound of shuffling feet behind the door and then it opened.

An old man stood there, or perhaps, thought Harry with sudden compassion, he might not be that old but aged by poverty. Behind him was a bare room with an iron bedstead.

"Are you Phil?" asked Harry.

"Right, guv. I'd ask you inside but there ain't nowheres to sit down."

Phil's face was marked by scabs and his clothes were ragged.

"Do you remember Reg Bolton?"

"That's over two years ago. Flash fellow, he were. Wouldn't spend the money to get his missus out of this rat hole. She said she was leaving him and he beat her to death. But he got loads o' villains to testify he was somewhere else at the time. Shame, it was."

"Did he know any grand people?"

"Naw, only villains."

"How old are you?" asked Harry.

"Fifty-five, come Tuesday."

"And how did you come to land up here?"

"The wife went off and left me. I adored my Elsie. Went to pieces. Lost me trade as a joiner. Shut up in the asylum, and when I got out I was done for. Just existed here ever since."

Harry could not bear to leave him. A voice in his head was screaming at him that he was surrounded by hundreds of other cases of dismal poverty and to leave Phil alone. But he found himself saying, "Come with me. I think I can find work for you. Have you belongings you can pack?"

"Got nothing but what you see."

"Come along."

Phil meekly shuffled down the stairs after them. Becket opened his mouth to protest and then shut it again as he remembered how Harry had saved him from a life of poverty after Becket had collapsed from hunger while working as a porter in Covent Garden.

The driver of the hansom told him that he wasn't going to allow Phil in his cab until Harry promised to pay extra.

"What is your name?" asked Harry.

"Phil Marshall."

"Well, Phil, first of all we need to get you cleaned up and get you some decent clothes."

"What can he do?" asked Becket.

"That cleaning woman is finishing work for us at the end of the week. Do you think you are fit enough to do some cleaning, Phil?"

"Reckon I could, guv. I feel a bit weak, mind."

"When did you last eat?"

"Maybe Tuesday."

"Dear me, and this is Friday. Becket, summon the doctor when we arrive. He'll need to treat those scabs."

Phil began to feel as if he had died and gone to heaven. A warm bath was run for him and Becket laid out clean underwear and a suit for him.

After that, he was checked by the doctor, who said the scabs were caused by untreated bedbug bites and malnutrition and suggested a gentle diet of soup and light meals to begin with.

Phil was given a small room in the basement and told to rest as much as possible.

He lay on the bed after Becket had gone, tears of gratitude pouring down his cheeks. He swore that from that day on, he would die for the captain if necessary.

Harry called on Rose later that day. She listened in alarm as he described the body fished out of the Thames and how they feared that Reg had been a hired assassin.

"But I think you will be safe now," he assured her. "A story has gone into all the newspapers that you held nothing back from the police."

"So I suppose you will feel free to go back to ignoring me."

"On the contrary," said Harry. "I have been remiss and

I do apologize. But you cannot have any social engagements in August. Everyone is away."

Rose bit her lip and then said in a small voice. "I'm bored."

"Then next week, I will take you for a drive if the weather is fine."

"I wish I were a man," raged Rose later to Daisy. "He can call at Scotland Yard any time he likes and be part of the investigation, but all I can do is sit here and rot and get letters from that dreary Mrs. Tremaine, oiling all over me in print. I am not interested in the fact that she and her dear husband have gone to Cromer on holiday."

Daisy brightened. "I am."

"Why, pray?"

"It would be interesting to go down to that village while the Tremaines have gone and ask around about them and about Dolly. See what we could find out."

"That is a splendid idea. I must find out how to get there."

"We could take one of the carriages."

"They've all got Pa's coat of arms on the panels. That would occasion comment. Better to travel by rail to the nearest town and take a carriage from there. We need not trouble to tell Aunt Phyllis where we are going. She is only concerned with ordering the servants around and eating vast quantities of food."

They took the train to Oxford and changed onto a local line and took another train to Moreton-in-Marsh, where they hired a waiting carriage to take them to Apton Magna.

"It is pleasant to be back in the country again," sighed Rose. "When all this is over, I shall go back north to see Bert and Sally."

"And how will you do that?" asked Daisy. "If your parents are at home, they are certainly not going to let you go all that way to see a mere village policeman."

"Perhaps the captain can arrange something," said Rose. "Oh, do look at that sweet cottage."

"All I see is the pump at the front for the water and no doubt the you-know-what will be out in the back garden. I can smell the cesspool from here."

"You have no romance in your soul," admonished Rose.

"I have memories of poverty in me soul," said Daisy.

"Don't say 'me.'"

They told the cabbie to wait for them at the entrance to the village. They had both decided to wear their plainest clothes.

A woman was sitting outside a cottage, holding a baby on her lap. "Excuse me," said Rose, "we were wondering if you could give us some information about the Tremaines."

The woman got to her feet and, disappearing inside the cottage, slammed the door behind her.

They met with the same lack of success at other cottages.

"Perhaps one of the more well-to-do residents would be more forthcoming," suggested Rose.

"There don't seen to be any," replied Daisy. "We've forgotten our village ways. We're too direct. We need someone friendly. Ask them something like where we can get a cup of tea, enter into conversation about the weather and so on, and then slide in some remark about the murder."

"That sounds a very good idea," said Rose. "That is, if we can find anyone amiable."

"I remember there was a cottage up by the rector's place. It looked in better shape than the others," said Daisy. "Why is the rector called 'doctor'?"

"Because he's a doctor of divinity. Remember that Gilbert and Sullivan opera? 'A doctor of divinity/Who resides in this vicinity.'"

The cottage they approached was small and thatched and made of Cotswold stone, unlike the red brick cottages of the other villagers.

It had a front garden crowded with flowers. They opened the gate and walked up the path. Rose knocked on the door.

A woman answered it. She looked washed-out and faded, as if some grim laundress had boiled her, mangled her and hung her out in strong sunlight to dry without ironing her first. Her simple muslin gown was creased, and the dry flaky skin of her long face, lined with wrinkles. Her eyes were of such a pale grey that they looked almost white and she wore her sparse grey hair under a crumpled linen cap.

"We are visiting the countryside and wondered whether there was anywhere in Apton Magna where we could get some refreshment," said Rose.

"Oh, there's nothing nearer than Moreton-in-Marsh. They do ever such a nice tea at the White Hart Royal. I remember being taken there by a gentleman friend when I was just a girl."

"Perhaps you would like to join us?" suggested Rose. "We have a carriage waiting at the end of the village. I am Lady Rose Summer and this is Miss Daisy Levine."

"That's is so kind of you. May I present myself? I am Miss Friendly." She plucked nervously at her gown. "I am not perhaps quite properly dressed."

"Nonsense," said Rose bracingly. "You will do very well."

"I don't know. Dear me. Afternoon tea! Such a luxury." She looked at them wistfully out of her pale eyes.

"I'll go and bring the carriage," said Daisy quickly, and ran off.

"Please step inside," said Miss Friendly. "The sun is very strong."

Rose followed her into a front parlour. There was very little furniture. There were light squares on the dingy wallpaper showing where pictures had once hung. Fallen on hard times, thought Rose, with a feeling of compassion.

"Do you live here alone, Miss Friendly?"

"Yes. Papa died ten years ago. He was rector of Saint Paul's before Dr. Tremaine. The church kindly allowed me to have this cottage."

Rose heard a rumble of carriage wheels outside.

"Ah, there is our carriage and Miss Levine. If you are ready, Miss Friendly?"

Seated in the pleasant gloom of the White Hart Royal over an enormous afternoon tea, Rose again felt a sharp pang of compassion as she watched Miss Friendly try not to gobble the food. The woman was obviously starving. Rose talked about the weather and about the beauties of the countryside until she saw that Miss Friendly's appetite was at last beginning to be satisfied.

"You must have been very upset over the news of Miss Tremaine's murder," she said.

"Oh, shocking. Very shocking. Poor Dolly. She often came to my little cottage. Such a beautiful girl. But very much a country girl. I always thought she would have been happy marrying a farmer, or someone like that, but her parents had such ambitions for her."

"I knew her in London," said Rose. "She was very unhappy."

"Of course. Lady Rose Summer! I saw your name in the newspapers. You found her. How awful. Yes, it was awful. But she must have been missing . . . Oh, I shouldn't gossip. Poor Dolly."

"My fiancé is a private detective," said Rose. "He is helping Scotland Yard to find the killer. Anything you can tell me would be of great help. Who was Dolly missing?"

"Roger Dallow."

"And who is this Roger Dallow?"

"He's the blacksmith's son. I think he and Dolly were very much in love."

"And is he in the village? May I speak to him?"

"Oh, he left, right after Dolly went up to London."

"And where did he go?"

"Nobody knows. You see, his father is a brutal man. I think that was the bond between Roger and Dolly. They were both bullied by their parents. I am sorry I cannot tell you any more. I assume that is why you invited me for tea."

"I could just as well have asked you these questions at your cottage," said Rose. "Do you find it difficult to make ends meet?"

For the first time colour appeared on Miss Friendly's pale cheeks. She hung her head. "Papa was fond of hunting and hunting is an expensive sport. When he died I had to sell his horses, my jewellery and pictures and furniture to pay his debts. The church charges me a low rent but I have nearly reached the point where I do not think I can go on paying it. Forgive me. Ladies should not talk of such things."

"Oh, we talk about anything," said Daisy. "Don't you worry about it."

"Can you sew?" asked Rose.

"Yes, I am a very good seamstress. Do not judge me by my clothes. It is a long time since I have been able to afford any material and . . . well . . . I gave up troubling about my appearance."

"Our lady's maid, Turner, is not very expert with a needle but is an amiable creature and I would not like to lose her." The main reason Rose liked Turner was because Turner never reported any of her doings to Lady Polly. "Perhaps you might consider working for me? You would have a comfortable room and board and you would not need to worry about the rent."

Miss Friendly burst into tears. Rose handed her a handkerchief and waited.

"It seems like a miracle," she gasped when she could.

"Then we will return to your cottage and you may pack a trunk and we will send a fourgon for the rest of your things later. My parents' secretary will advise the church of your leaving."

Lady Rose should really have put Miss Friendly in a second-class compartment, which is where servants normally travelled. But the woman looked so frail, she decided to buy her a first-class ticket. Full of food, Miss Friendly fell asleep as soon as the train moved off.

"That was right decent of you," said Daisy.

"I think when this murder is solved that I should get involved in charity work. My parents cannot object. It is quite fashionable to do so."

"Do we have enough work for her?" asked Daisy. "We're always getting new clothes."

"There is plenty of work. Servants' clothes often need to be altered. Hats need to be trimmed. I will make sure she is kept busy."

Aunt Phyllis started to complain about the employment of Miss Friendly, but Rose silenced her with a haughty glare, and saying, "You have no right to question who I engage."

To Rose's relief the housekeeper, Mrs. Holt, actually welcomed the newcomer, privately planning to have several of her own gowns made over. Miss Friendly was given a small bedchamber off the second landing and shown the sewing-room in one of the attics.

Matthew Jarvis called on her to get the details of whom to notify in the church and where to send the fourgon. To Miss Friendly's amazed delight, she found she was to get a salary as well.

Then the housekeeper, under Rose's instructions, presented Miss Friendly with two bolts of cloth.

"Lady Rose says you might want to begin by making some frocks for yourself."

The next day, Miss Friendly began to work, the sewing-machine humming under her clever fingers, stopping occasionally to caress the rich cloth. As she worked, she began to search her mind for everything she knew about the Tremaines.

Perhaps she had forgotten something that might help Lady Rose's fiancé with the investigation.

Harry called on Rose that evening. He listened carefully while she told him about the blacksmith's son. "I'll tell Kerridge. He might have followed the Tremaines to London. I would like to speak to this woman myself. I will go to Apton Magna tomorrow."

"That will not be necessary. I have engaged her as a seamstress. She is here."

"How did that come about?"

"She was so poor and so hungry. Besides, she will be of use."

Harry thought of his rescue of Phil. How like he and Rose really were. He wanted suddenly to tell her that they should start again, that perhaps they could deal very well together, but Rose had risen to ring the bell and ask a footman to fetch Miss Friendly.

She came in and sat down timidly on the very edge of a chair. "I am Captain Cathcart," Harry began, "and I believe you have supplied Lady Rose with some very interesting information about the blacksmith's son."

"Only that he and Dolly were very much in love. I believe they used to meet in secret. You can't keep much quiet in a village. The rector complained to the blacksmith and the blacksmith gave Roger a terrible beating. That was just before they took Dolly to London."

"Miss Tremaine gave Lady Rose a note saying she was running away. It is possible that she knew where this Roger was and was going to join him. On the other hand, he could have killed her. What sort of fellow was he?"

"Very strong. Curly black hair and quite tall. He told someone in the village that he was running off to London."

"Would it be possible to find a photograph of him?"

"I shouldn't think so, sir. I cannot remember anyone in the village having a camera."

"I'll get Kerridge on to this," said Harry. "Thank you, Miss Friendly."

She curtsied and left.

"You should not have risked going to Apton Magna without telling me," said Harry.

"How could I tell you? You are never here."

"I do have a telephone, as you well know."

"I do not like not having the freedom of a man," said Rose. "You are able to visit Scotland Yard any time you like and find out the latest developments."

"I could wish you were more conventional for your own safety."

"One could hardly call *you* conventional."

"True, but it is different for a man."

"I sometimes feel like cancelling our engagement and marrying Sir Peter."

He glared at her in outrage. "That would be a marriage in name only."

"As this is an engagement in name only," retorted Rose.

The much-goaded Harry seized her in his arms and kissed her hard on the lips. When she reeled back after he had released her, he said, "I am sorry. I should not have done that. But you are *infuriating!*"

And with that, he turned and left the room.

FIVE

✠

The accepted man is in duty bound to spend most of his leisure with his
intended bride. He must not go off for a sojourn abroad while she is
spending some weeks by the sea in England, unless she has expressed a
wish to that effect. It would be a considerable "snub" to her to do so. . . .
This almost always means that the man has been entrapped into a pro-
posal, and would willingly retreat if he possibly could.

— MRS. HUMPHREY

Rose almost telephoned Harry to cancel the outing. That kiss
had left her feeling weak and shaken. Somehow, she could
not even bring herself to tell Daisy about it. Also, Daisy was
volubly looking forward so much to the outing.

Rose knew the rigid rules of society were relaxing. A gentleman was no longer expected to ask the parents' permission
first if he wanted to pay his addresses to their daughter. Only
sticklers for the old ways such as her own parents and no
doubt the mercenary Tremaines expected the old ways to be
followed.

She looked down at the small engagement ring on her
finger. She had bought it herself out of her pin money,
Harry having seemingly forgotten that he was expected to
supply one.

The weather held fine for the day of the outing. Rose was torn between "armouring" herself in a new white lace gown with a high-boned collar and settling for comfort. Comfort won. Her maid dressed her in a divided tweed skirt and a striped blouse. Although the day showed every sign of becoming hot, Rose put on a tweed jacket and wore a straw boater on her glossy hair.

Daisy had been up very early, trying on outfit after outfit to impress Becket. When she finally appeared to join Rose in a purple silk gown embellished with purple lace, Rose exclaimed in horror.

"We are not making calls, Daisy. You will need to find something informal." Rose rang for the maid and soon a rather sulky Daisy was attired in a simple skirt and white blouse. She protested volubly against wearing a straw boater like Rose, and only because she was told the captain was waiting for her did Rose allow Daisy to get away with wearing a cart-wheel of a straw hat covered in so many flowers that from above she looked like a neatly tended garden bed.

Rose was nervous at seeing Harry again. He should not have taken such liberties with her.

But Harry looked as cool and distant as he usually did. He helped Rose into the passenger seat of his Rolls and Daisy and Becket got into the back.

"I thought we might find somewhere pleasant on the upper reaches of the river," said Harry. He meant the Thames. To a Londoner, there was only one river.

Rose gave a curt nod and settled back against the red leather seat. The car purred off. Daisy began to chatter to Becket, and Rose envied her free and easy manner.

I know nothing of men, she thought bleakly. I do not understand them. I wish I had brothers.

At last Harry spoke. "You haven't seen anyone suspicious hanging about, I hope?"

"No one at all," said Rose, "although we have hardly been out of doors except for our journey to Apton Magna."

"Do not go anywhere like that without letting me know about it first."

"It is rather hard, since you are always busy."

"As I told you, I am not going to take on any more work until this case is finished. Has your Miss Friendly come up with any more gems of information?"

"No, but she says she is trying to remember every little thing. Any news of Mr. Cyril Banks?"

"He is in Scotland at the moment. Shooting party."

"Do you think he might be the murderer?"

"I do not know. He is incredibly vain. There are some unsavoury stories about him."

"Such as?"

"When he was staying with Lord Berrow in the country, he was accused of molesting a servant girl. He denied the whole thing. Despite the fact that Berrow's servants claimed that he had indeed forced his way into the girl's bedchamber, Berrow backed Cyril, saying the girl was a slut. He dismissed her. Her parents complained to the church and to the lord lieutenant, but nothing came of it."

"Why?"

"Because there is one law for the rich and one for the poor. Just be grateful for your privileged position, Lady Rose. The unconventional risks you take might end in disaster if you were of a lower class."

"So Berrow and Cyril Banks are friends? And both wished to marry Dolly. Don't you find that odd?"

"Yes, I do rather, and quite sinister."

"What is sinister about it?"

Harry bit his lip. He knew Berrow, like Cyril, had a foul reputation. It had crossed his mind that perhaps Berrow, had he managed to woo and marry Dolly, might have allowed his friend access to her.

"Just that they are both unsavoury characters."

They drove on down leafy roads, the trees heavy with the weight of summer, the leaves a dark and dusty green.

"You should have worn a veil," said Harry as a cloud of dust rose up about the car from an unmetalled country road.

"I'll hold a handkerchief over my face."

As they cruised along beside the river, the usual picnic argument started up. Every time Harry looked like stopping, either Rose or Daisy would cry out, "No, not there! Try a little farther on."

At last Harry rebelled and came to a stop by an area of green grass surrounded by willow trees. "Here and no argument," he said, "or it will be midnight before we eat."

Becket lifted a large hamper out of the boot and then began to pump up a small spirit stove.

Harry spread rugs on the grass and Rose and Daisy helped Becket lift out dishes, glasses and food from the hamper.

They drank champagne and ate delicacies from Fortnum and Mason such as grouse in aspic while the river chuckled past over the willow trees and the moving leaves of the other trees around their green oasis on the river bank sent flickering shadows over their faces.

When the meal was finished, Harry said to Rose, "Walk a little with me. I have something for you."

He helped her to her feet and they strolled away through the trees watched by the ever-hopeful Becket and Daisy.

He finally stopped and pulled a little jeweller's box out of his pocket. "I should have bought you a ring before this. Most remiss of me."

Rose opened the box. A large and beautiful diamond set in white gold glittered up at her, throwing rainbow prisms of light across her astonished face.

"This is too much," she said. "I cannot accept it. It is not as if we are really engaged."

"I wish you would keep it as a memento of all our adventures. The diamond was a present to me from someone in South Africa."

He took her hand in his and slid off the little engagement ring she had bought herself. Rose stood frozen as he slid his ring onto her finger. "Please take it . . . Rose."

She suddenly smiled up at him. "Yes, I will. Thank you. I think we could be friends after all."

He tucked her arm in his and they walked on. "You must admit we are a very unusual pair. The misfits of society. Just like Kerridge."

"Is Mr. Kerridge a misfit?"

"Indeed he is. He would like to see all the aristocracy strung up from lamp-posts with himself manning the barricades at some people's revolution."

"Why? We have always been kind to him."

"I can see his point. Any time he has to interview one of us, he is threatened with losing his job. 'My friend the Prime Minister will hear of this.' That sort of thing."

"Mostly I accept my position in life," said Rose slowly. "One is immured from the sufferings of humanity. But when I rescued Miss Friendly, I was almost ashamed of myself for having chosen one easily grateful genteel lady who will not cause me any trouble when there are others, hundreds and thousands, even more deserving."

"I felt the same way when I rescued Phil. Did I tell you about Phil?"

Rose listened while he described his visit to Bermondsey. Then she said, "When I reach my majority I will have my own money. I wish to set up a charity."

"Let me know," said Harry, "and I will contribute."

They walked back to join Becket and Daisy. Becket was making tea. Rose showed Daisy her ring and Daisy glanced at Becket, who sent her a covert wink.

They were all happy and at ease with each other when they finally drove back to London.

But then, just as they were travelling along the Great West Road, Harry asked, "How do you find my Aunt Phyllis?"

"She has very taking ways. Most of our servants are still at the town house and yet she moved in a staff of her own. She orders things like gowns and books and charges them to my parents' account."

"You must be mistaken," said Harry. "You are talking about my mother's sister. She was so eager to be of help."

"Of course she was," said Rose. "I am sure she would eagerly go anywhere for free lodging."

"Take that back!"

"No!"

In the back, Becket and Daisy exchanged alarmed glances.

"I have always found her charming and amiable," said Harry.

"Indeed?" Rose's voice dripped sarcasm. "And when did you last see her?"

"Not for some years."

"So there you are! You do not know her at all."

"I do not believe you."

"Are you calling me a liar?"

"Just misinformed."

By the time they drove up to the town house, Rose and Harry were not on speaking terms. Rose wanted to give Harry back his ring but did not wish to make a scene on the street.

"I would invite you in," she said coldly, "but I am sure you are anxious to get to your own home. Come, Daisy."

Daisy threw an anguished glance over her shoulder at Becket and trailed inside after Rose.

Mrs. Holt, the housekeeper, was waiting for them. Aunt Phyllis had brought her own housekeeper, but Mrs. Holt had told the intruder not to interfere at all in the running of the house.

"May I have a word with you, my lady?"

"By all means." Rose unpinned her hat. "What is the matter?"

Mrs. Holt lowered her voice. "It's Lady Phyllis. My lady has given Miss Friendly so many gowns and hats to alter that I swear poor Miss Friendly has been working all night."

"I'll see to it." Rose marched all the way up to the sewing-room.

Miss Friendly was bent over the sewing-machine. She stopped when she saw Rose, got to her feet and stumbled, holding on to the table for support. There were purple shadows under her eyes.

"Stop everything," commanded Rose. "You are not to do any work for Lady Phyllis." She rang the bell and when a footman answered it, she told him to fetch Lady Phyllis's lady's maid. When the maid arrived, Rose told her to take away all Lady Phyllis's hats and garments and then said, "Lady Phyllis will be leaving immediately. Miss Friendly, you are not to do any more work for the next two days. Go to your room and relax, or go out for a walk."

Rose marched back downstairs and into the study, where Matthew Jarvis was working.

"Ah, Lady Rose," he said, "I have just received a wire. My lord and lady will be returning at the end of the week. They wish you to go to Stacey Court as soon as possible."

"Very well," said Rose. Let rotten Harry Cathcart do the investigation himself. "Mr. Jarvis, I should be grateful if you would inform Lady Phyllis's butler that she and her staff are leaving as soon as possible. By as soon as possible, I mean tomorrow morning at the latest."

The outraged Lady Phyllis shouted and protested when she received the news, but all she got was a blistering lecture from Rose on her abuse of the household and its staff.

Lady Phyllis telephoned Harry, who replied that he could not contradict Lady Rose's decision as it was her home. But he was furious with Rose and thought her action was that of petty spite.

By the end of the week, Becket could not bear it any longer. "You know, sir, that you paid me to find out gossip from the Running Footman?"

"Yes, Becket, and did you find out anything relating to the murders?"

"No, sir, it's just that I could not help overhearing your argument with Lady Rose over Lady Phyllis."

Harry's face hardened. "And what has that to do with anything?"

"It's just that some of your aunt's staff also drink in the Running Footman."

"I repeat: What has that to do with anything?"

"Lady Phyllis's nickname is Lady Sponge."

"What!"

"It seems that Lady Phyllis likes to be invited into other people's homes and once there, she costs them a lot of money. Furthermore, she usually takes with her as many servants as she can so that she is spared the expense of feeding them."

"Are you sure?"

"Some other servants joined our gossip. They, too, remember visits from Lady Phyllis. One said she had only been invited for tea and yet she turned up with all her baggage and servants and claimed that she had been invited to stay. It took a couple of months to get rid of her."

Harry ran a hand through his thick hair. "Oh dear. I had better visit Lady Rose."

But when they arrived at the town house, it was to find only a caretaker and his wife in residence. Harry was told that the whole family was now at Stacey Court. He telephoned the earl, confidently expecting to be invited down, but it was Matthew who answered his call and told him that Lady Rose had given instructions that Captain Harry Cathcart was to be told she was "not at home."

"Not at home" was society's snub. It was a way of saying, "I don't want to see you."

He sat down and wrote a heartfelt apology to Rose. Her father read it and decided not to show it to his daughter. Sir Peter Petrey was due back from Scotland soon. If only Rose would break off her engagement to this eccentric captain, Sir Peter would be so eligible and Rose seemed to like him. The earl threw Harry's letter on the fire and decided to invite Peter to come on a visit.

Harry, on receiving no reply from Rose, thought she was childish and ungracious. It never dawned on him that such an independent spirit as Rose Summer would have her mail read by her father.

As the weeks passed and there were no new leads on the murder of Dolly Tremaine, Harry, still smarting over what he saw as Rose's rejection of him, began to take on new cases and immersed himself in his work.

As autumn crept over the English countryside and the smoky bonfire air hung over the bare frosty fields, the earl and countess began to make preparations to remove to London for the Little Season.

Only Daisy felt as if she had been condemned to years and years of Sundays where nothing ever happened. Sir Peter had come on an extended visit and Rose seemed to enjoy his light-hearted company very much.

It was a damp drizzly day when the cavalcade of carriages and fourgons arrived at the town house. The sight of the earl and his family and servants moving from the country to the town was like watching the procession of some minor foreign royalty.

Smoke swirled down from chimney-cowls and the buildings were black with soot. As they arrived, the lamplighter with his long brass pole was making his journey around the square like some magician, raising his pole and sending another golden globe of light out into the dusk, leaving behind him as he passed from lamp-post to lamp-post, a warm constellation of minor planets.

Rose felt heavy of heart as she stepped down from the carriage. London, again. London, where the infuriating Harry Cathcart had no doubt forgotten about her.

The only thing to raise her spirits was the thought that at

balls and parties she would no doubt see the Honourable Cyril Banks. Some detecting was just what she needed to make her feel that her life was not totally useless.

She was to have the opportunity of seeing Cyril sooner than she expected. The next day, having accepted the invitation to afternoon tea at the Barrington-Bruces while she was still in the country, Lady Polly set out, accompanied by Rose and Daisy, her own lady's maid, Rose's lady's maid, and two footmen.

Lady Polly wished to show off her new hat. It was not really new but one that Miss Friendly had refurbished. Lady Polly had quite forgotten how much she had objected to Rose's hiring Miss Friendly in her absence and now considered the employing of the seamstress to have been all her own idea.

Lady Polly's round figure was covered in a large sable coat and round her neck was a sable stole. Her felt hat was trimmed with sable fur and on her small feet were fur boots. She felt very chic and did not know that her daughter thought she looked like some exotic beast in a cage at London Zoo.

Rose herself was wrapped in a long fox coat but with a small fur hat perched rakishly over her curls. Daisy beside her, wearing a squirrel coat, felt its warmth banishing the cold of the day and wondered if she would ever see Becket again.

When they arrived at the large white house in Kensington, they left their coats and entered the drawing-room in their tea-gowns. A fire was blazing on the hearth, but there was a large embroidered fire-screen in front of it and the room was cold.

Rose recognized Cyril immediately. She waited for him to

settle down so that she could get a chance to talk to him about Dolly. But she had to wait quite a time. The duties of a gentleman at five-o'clock tea were onerous. He had to carry teacups about, hand sugar, cream, cakes or muffins, all the time keeping up a flow of small talk. He had to rise every time a lady entered or left the room.

At last he found a chair beside Rose and settled himself with a sigh. "Thought I was never going to get anything to eat."

"There is plenty left," said Rose. "Ladies do not eat, you know."

"Except for your companion."

Rose looked to where Daisy was ruining her gloves by putting a muffin dripping with butter into her mouth.

"You must be as distressed as I am about the death of poor Miss Tremaine," began Rose.

"Oh, that? Beastly business. I was grilled at Scotland Yard. Can you believe it?"

"How too frightful for you," said Rose, smiling into his eyes.

"I say, that fiancé of yours was there! Aren't you ashamed of him being in trade?"

This was insolence, but Rose chose to ignore it. "His work certainly takes him away from me a lot."

"If I were your fiancé," said Cyril, "I would stick by your side the whole time."

Rose rapped his arm with her fan and giggled, "Oh, sir, you flatter me."

Cyril eyes brightened. Rose was a considerable heiress and rumour had it that her engagement was shortly about to be broken. She was hardly ever seen out in society with her fiancé, and the gossips had said that he had never even visited her when she was in the country.

"I do miss Dolly," said Rose, looking suddenly sad. "I wonder why she was running away?"

"I think I can tell you that," said Cyril. "I think she was one of Sappho's sisters."

Rose stared at him, puzzled. What had Dolly to do with Greece, and why was Cyril leering at her in that odd way? She remembered the lines of a Lord Byron poem: "What men call gallantry, and gods adultery/Is much more common where the climate's sultry." He was always writing about Greece and he did have some poem about Sappho. Had there been some scandal? Had Dolly been in love with a married man? Her thoughts raced round and round at the same busy rate that had once animated the dead squirrels of Daisy's coat.

"I do not understand you, sir."

"Oh, never mind," said Cyril hurriedly, realizing if Rose did actually understand him, she might think he was calling her a lesbian as well. He fetched up a sigh. "Deuced pretty girl, what?"

"Yes, indeed and so sad. Did she ever say anything to you about being threatened by anyone?"

"No, on the contrary, my friend Berrow was about to make her an offer."

"Lord Berrow is quite old, is he not?"

"Stout fellow. In his prime."

"I am surprised to hear you speak so well of him when it looked as if he was about to succeed where you had failed."

"Believe me, Lady Rose, our friendship will survive anything. Now, I do not like to hear about murder from those pretty lips of yours."

"I wonder, sir, if you would mind asking Mrs. Barrington-Bruce to remove the fire-screen?"

Cyril darted off. When he returned it was to find his place had been taken by Sir Peter, who had just arrived.

"When I came in," said Peter, "you were flirting with that dreadful toad, Banks."

"I was trying to find out information about Dolly," whispered Rose.

"He is an awful pill. Do you think he killed her? He's vicious, I think. There was some scandal."

"Oh, here he comes," said Rose, raising her fan. "Do talk about something else."

Daisy slipped from the room. On entering the house she had seen a telephone in the hall. She had wanted to phone Becket to tell him she was back in town, but Matthew had gone on a week's leave and the study door was locked. She looked nervously about.

The hall boy, who had been half asleep in his chair, stirred himself. "You looking for the Jericho, madam?"

"No, I wonder if I might use the telephone?"

"Is it all right with Mrs. Barrington-Bruce?"

"Oh, yes."

"That's all right, then. I'm just going down to the kitchen. If anyone needs me, ring the bell."

Daisy waited until the green baize door had closed behind him and then picked up the receiver and asked the operator to connect her.

To her relief, Becket answered the phone. "It's me, Daisy," she whispered. "Why hasn't the captain called?"

"He did not know you were back. He wrote a letter of apology to Lady Rose but she did not reply."

"Her father reads all her post. He probably destroyed it. The captain should call."

"I'll tell him. We are going to Oxford tomorrow. The captain wishes to talk to Mr. Jeremy Tremaine."

"I wish we could go with you. I wish—"

Daisy heard the drawing-room door upstairs begin to open and hurriedly replaced the receiver.

"I sometimes wonder if perhaps I should be focusing my attention on Lord Berrow," said Rose to Peter.

"He's even more foul than Cyril."

"That is interesting. A murderer surely must be a foul person. Perhaps I will flirt with him a little when I next see him."

"Isn't your fiancé annoyed when he sees you flirting with other men?"

"Oh, no, he will understand it is all part of research."

"And what does your oh-so-frequently-absent captain think of me?"

Rose looked at him in surprise. "He knows you are my friend. You are famous in society for being available to escort ladies who have been left stranded by their escorts."

He laughed. "What a reputation to have! Do you not care for me a little?"

"You are a flirt, sir. Of course I value your friendship. Why is Daisy grimacing and winking at me?"

"Miss Levine, may I say, is a most unusual companion."

"Excuse me." Rose got up and made her way to the corner of the room where Daisy was standing. "Why are you making all those funny faces?"

"I phoned Becket to say I was back in town," whispered Daisy. "The captain sent you a full letter of apology. Your father must have torn it up."

Rose was suddenly furiously angry. She knew that her

father would bluster and deny that she had been sent any such letter.

"You know, Daisy, I sometimes feel like marrying *anyone* just to have my own home and freedom." Rose looked thoughtfully across the room at Peter.

"Bad idea," said Daisy. "Men you marry can turn into heavy fathers."

"How would you know that, pray?"

"Observation."

Daisy watched anxiously as Rose went back to join Peter and saw the ease with which Rose chatted and smiled at him. But the captain would surely call that evening.

Harry arrived home late. Becket helped him out of his coat and told him about the destroyed letter.

"I will see Lady Rose tomorrow," said Harry.

"We are leaving early for Oxford, sir," Becket reminded him.

"I shall call on her when we return."

Rose was prepared for bed by her maid. She picked up a book to read before going to sleep and then crossed to the window, parted the curtains and looked down into the square.

Two men were standing over by the gardens, black silhouettes in the night. Something made her let the curtain fall and turn off the gaslight. She returned to the window and parted the curtains an inch and looked down again. The two men had moved into a pool of lamplight. Cyril Banks and Lord Berrow. As she watched, they both looked up at the house.

She dropped the curtain quickly and stood there, her heart beating hard, suddenly frightened. Where was Harry?

The next morning, Harry parked his motor car at Paddington Station and he and Becket took the train to Oxford. They sat in the dining-car and ordered breakfast as the train gave a great hiss and moved out of the station into a black and rainy morning.

When the train stopped at Slough, Harry suddenly said, "I really do not know what to do about this engagement of mine."

"To Lady Rose?"

"Who else? Perhaps, if I had not gone along with her plan, she might have enjoyed India and met some handsome officer."

"I think Lady Rose would be made unhappy by a conventional husband," said Becket. "If I may make so bold, sir, I think you and my lady are ideally suited."

"Nonsense. We would fight the whole time."

Harry stared gloomily out onto the platform. Opposite was a tin advertisement: "They come as a boon and a blessing to men, the Pickwick, the Owl, and the Waverley pen."

"I wonder who thinks up these advertisements," said Harry. "Some failed poet?" And Becket knew the subject was closed.

But at a telephone-box at Oxford Station, Harry telephoned Matthew and asked which social engagement Rose had for that evening.

"A fancy dress party at the Sowerbys," said Matthew.

"Tell Lady Rose I shall be there to escort her." Harry rang off. "I shall be going to a fancy dress party tonight, Becket. Do I have fancy dress?"

"No, but perhaps we could improvise."

They walked down from the station and climbed into a hansom carriage. "Is Phil doing well?" asked Harry.

"Yes, he is very diligent. The house has never been so clean."

"How does he pass his leisure time?"

"He reads. He enjoys books."

"I am thinking of starting a charity to help the poor of the East End. Perhaps we will get Phil involved. Instead of lords and ladies playing the part of bountiful benefactors, perhaps someone like Phil would be good at finding out the truly deserving. We have more than enough money now. Do I pay you enough, Becket?"

"At the moment, yes."

"What does that mean?"

"Would it be possible to continue to work for you were I married?"

"You, Becket?"

"You must have noticed my fondness for Miss Levine."

"We will see. Lady Rose without Daisy would be completely unprotected."

"Perhaps the ideal solution would be for you to marry Lady Rose and protect her yourself," said Becket boldly.

"That's enough, Becket. I will consider your problem, but for the moment I wish to hear no more about it."

St. Edwin's was one of the lesser Oxford colleges, having been built on Gothic lines in the last century. They asked for Mr. Jeremy Tremaine at the porter's lodge and were escorted across to a stair off the main quadrangle.

"First-floor landing, sirs," said the porter and left them.

They mounted the shallow stone stairs and knocked at the door on the first landing.

Harry had somehow hoped that the Tremaine family, driven by thwarted ambition, had murdered their own daughter. He had decided against the rector and his wife, however, which left the son.

But the man who answered the door to them looked as if he could not hurt a fly. All the looks had gone to Dolly. Despite his youth, Jeremy was tall, thin and slightly stooped. He had a yellowish skin, like tallow, and wore spectacles on the end of his nose. He was dressed in a severe black suit and a white shirt with a high starched collar. His dusty fair hair was already thinning. Over his suit, he was huddled into a dog-hair rug.

Harry introduced himself. "Come in," said Jeremy. "Excuse my dress, but the lazy scout has only just made up the fire. May I offer you something? Sherry?"

They both refused. Becket took a chair by the door and Harry sat down in an armchair facing the one into which Jeremy had just lowered his long thin form.

"Is it about my sister's murder?" asked Jeremy.

"Yes, we still have no new clues. Have you any idea who could have done this?"

"I have thought and thought."

"It must have been someone she knew," said Harry. "She must have put on that fancy dress to show someone."

"Perhaps she wanted to show it to Lady Rose and was attacked by some madman in the park."

"An intellectual madman," said Harry dryly, "to take the trouble to arrange her like the Lady of Shalott."

"I've thought about that," said Jeremy eagerly. "What if the whole effect was an accident? What if the murderer, horrified at what he had done, simply, well, laid her out, as it were?"

"Perhaps," said Harry. "There was talk that Miss Tremaine was fond of a local blacksmith's son, Roger Dallow."

Jeremy gave a scornful laugh. "Village gossip. I know where that came from. That old maid, Miss Friendly, always mooning about the place and dreaming of romance. Every boy and man for miles around was fascinated by Dolly, but she did not encourage any of them."

"Have you any idea what became of Roger?"

"He ran away. I know that. His father is a brutal man, so nobody was surprised."

"And he never wrote to your sister or tried to communicate with her in any way? Becket, pray come nearer the fire. You must be frozen over there."

Jeremy gave a sour laugh. "As far as I know, Dallow was illiterate. He was keen to attend school, I'll say that for him, but his father kept him working at the smithy."

Harry repressed a sigh. This whole journey had turned out to be a waste of time. He had learned that Jeremy had spent the summer in Greece and had waited eagerly for the Michaelmas term at Oxford to begin in the autumn. He could think of nothing more to ask him and he and Becket took their leave.

As the train approached London, he looked down at the little houses with their neat suburban gardens and said to Becket, "I wonder what it would be like to live in one of those little houses, free from the pressures of society."

Becket followed his gaze and repressed a smile. "Those are the homes of the lower middle classes, sir. You would find snobbery and social rules are as rigid as they are in high society. Some people even imagine escaping to a cottage in the country. The vicar and his wife would call and so pigeonhole them into the correct social stratum. The news of the incomers would go round the village and they would only receive calls from people on their own social level and be subjected to all the petty tyrannies of snobbery. But cheer up, sir. The aristocratic male does have freedom. If he does not conform to the rules of society, he is regarded as eccentric. If he is very rich and marriageable, then he is regarded as Byronic."

"I did not know you were such a cynic, Becket."

"Merely an observer of the world."

There was a sudden huge bang and the carriage in which they were sitting tumbled over on one side.

The shattered gas lamps plunged the carriage into darkness, but there was still the ominous hiss of gas.

"Climb on my back, Becket, and open the door up there," shouted Harry. "One spark and this place will be in flames. Where are you, man?"

"Here, sir."

"Right! Up on my back, fast!"

Becket struggled until he got a firm hold on Harry's coat and hauled himself up.

He struggled and managed to jerk the window down by its leather strap, and leaned out.

"Out you go!" shouted Harry.

"But, sir. How will you get out?"

"Get on with it, man."

Becket crawled down the side of the train. The air was full of wails, shrieks and cries.

Harry gave a great leap and grasped hold of the edge of the window. With a superhuman effort he pulled himself out and slithered down to join Becket just as a great fireball exploded near the engine. Flames began to engulf the train.

"To the end of the train," panted Harry. "We may be able to pull some people out."

They ran down the train away from the fire. They struggled up to doors and got them open, dragging men, women and children out, shouting to them to run clear of the train.

At last, the wooden carriages, combined with gaslight, went up one after the other in explosions of flame.

Harry and Becket struggled clear and watched in horror as the flaming train lying on its side began to slide down the embankment. With a great crashing roar, it tumbled down onto the houses beneath.

Harry sat down and buried his face in his hands. His leg, injured in the Boer War, was throbbing but he hardly felt the pain.

And then the rain began to pour down, streaking their sooty faces with white lines, running down like tears.

Still they sat there, master and servant, numb with shock.

At last Harry struggled to his feet and helped Becket up. The air was full of the sound of the bells of fire engines. And then there was silence.

They walked to where the head of the train had been. It had collided full on with the up train, and despite the rain, the up train was burning from end to end.

Rose, dressed as Columbine, descended the stairs. "How pretty you look!" exclaimed Lady Polly.

"Thank you. Where is Captain Cathcart?"

"Nowhere, as usual," snapped her mother. "We will need to go without him."

The earl and countess were attired in eighteenth-century dress.

Rose's heart sank. She knew she looked well in her costume and had been looking forward to seeing Harry admire it.

She felt a ball of hurt somewhere in her stomach. He did not care for her, not even a little bit. He had snubbed her again. How the débutantes would titter and gossip behind their fans when she arrived alone.

As they were about to leave, Peter called. "I wanted to show you my costume," he said, swinging a black coat from his shoulders. Despite her hurt, Rose began to laugh. He was dressed as harlequin.

"As my fiancé has not put in an appearance and we match, I would be honoured if you would escort me."

"Delighted and honoured," said Peter.

The earl and countess exchanged little smiles. Peter was eligible and very suitable. The captain was not. Surely Rose would break the engagement now.

SIX

✠

For talk six times with the same single lady,
And you may get the wedding dresses ready.

— LORD BYRON

A stonemason who had been rescued from a third-class carriage along with his wife and two children had demanded at
the time to know the name of his rescuer. Harry had simply
smiled and run off to try to rescue someone else. But Becket
had shouted back, "Captain Harry Cathcart."

One of the stonemason's sons had a broken arm. Reporters haunting the nearby hospitals began to hear of some
hero who had gone from carriage to carriage rescuing people. They came upon the stonemason as he was leaving the
hospital with his family, his son's arm in a splint. He told
them that the lives of himself and his family had been saved
by a Captain Harry Cathcart.

Daisy slipped out the following day for a walk. She was very
troubled. Peter and Rose had won first prize for their costumes.
Everyone was talking about what a handsome pair they made.

She walked until she reached Piccadilly. Outside the new
Ritz Hotel, a news-vendor was shouting, "Read all abaht it!
Hero of train crash."

Daisy was about to walk on when she recognized Harry's face on the front page. She fumbled in her reticule for her change purse and bought a copy and went into Green Park where she could read it in peace.

The photograph of Harry had been taken a year before at a charity fund-raising garden party. Daisy read in growing horror about the train crash. Becket was referred to only as Harry's manservant. He could have been killed, she thought, the newspaper trembling in her hands, oblivious to the black ink that was soiling her gloves.

Various friends telephoned the earl to exclaim over Harry's bravery. He told his wife.

"Perhaps we will say nothing of this to Rose," said Lady Polly. "It is better at the moment that she should think he did not care enough about her to attend last night."

At that moment, Rose entered the drawing-room carrying a letter and a little jeweller's box.

"I am returning Captain's Cathcart's ring," she said. "I have written him a letter asking him to release me from the engagement."

"It's all for the best," said Lady Polly. "I'll get John footman to take it straight to him. Matthew shall send an announcement to the newspapers straight away."

Harry had told Becket to take the day off. Phil, proud of his temporary position as butler, was answering the door and telling the press in strangulated tones of refinement that the captain was "not at home."

Phil was unrecognizable as the wreck that Harry had first

brought home. His skin was clear and healthy and his figure erect. He loved his room and his books. He wished he'd been on that train with the guv'nor and maybe had a chance to rescue him.

He answered the door again, prepared to send another reporter away, but it was the earl's footman who stood there. He handed Phil the letter and the little jeweller's box. "My Lady Rose requested me to give these to Captain Cathcart."

Phil took the letter and box in to where Harry was sitting at his desk in the parlour.

"From Lady Rose," said Phil.

Harry looked bleakly at the letter and then at the jeweller's box. "Thank you, Phil, that will be all."

"Right, guv." Phil backed out of the room as if before royalty.

Harry opened the jeweller's box. The ring he had given Rose sparkled up at him.

He broke open the seal on the letter. He read: "Dear Captain Cathcart, As you have once again shown your indifference to me by failing to escort me last night or even to send an apology, I am terminating our engagement. This will be best for both of us. Yours sincerely, Rose Summer."

"The hell with her," said Harry out loud. "Now I need never be hurt again!"

Daisy hurried upstairs, clutching the *Evening News*. She erupted into Rose's sitting-room, crying, "You'll never believe it!"

"What is it, Daisy?" Rose was slumped in an armchair by the fire.

"It's about the captain. He's a hero. Oh, if only they had got Becket's name!"

"Let me see that newspaper."

Daisy handed it over. Rose read the story of Harry's bravery with increasing horror.

She turned a white face up to Daisy. "I have just written to him sending his ring back and Matthew has sent a notice to the *Times* cancelling our engagement."

"Why?" shrieked Daisy.

"Because he did not attend me last night. I thought he was snubbing me."

"Cancel the notice!"

"I can't," said Rose dismally. "It's done. It's for the best."

"You fool," said Daisy bitterly. "You bloody little fool." She burst into tears and fled from the room.

Rose was in more disgrace than she had been when her photograph had appeared once on the front page of the *Daily Mail* showing her attending a suffragette rally. She had jilted England's latest hero. The announcement had appeared in the *Times* and the gossipy papers had recognized a story. All the facts of Dolly's murder were dragged up again. A nasty bit of speculation began to run through society that someone as unstable as Lady Rose Summer might have killed Dolly herself in a fit of jealous rage.

Daisy was angry with her, wondering if she would ever see Becket again. Three days after the announcement Daisy felt she could not bear it any longer and slipped out of the house and took a hansom to Chelsea.

When Becket answered the door, Daisy burst into tears and fell into his arms.

He drew her gently inside, saying, "Please don't cry. We'll think of something."

At last, Daisy, fortified with hot gin, gulped and said, "My lady is in such disgrace. Some people are beginning to think she might have murdered Dolly herself."

"But that is ridiculous!"

"I know. But mud like that sticks. Invitations have been cancelled. Lady Polly is in fits. It's all her fault for encouraging Rose to break off the engagement, but of course she puts the blame for everything all on Rose."

"It is a pity there is no other gentleman in Lady Rose's life."

"Why?"

"Because society would assume that she was so much in love with this other fellow that she had to ditch the captain."

"There's only Sir Peter and we both know what he is."

"That might be gossip. We may be mistaken."

"Don't think so."

"Then perhaps Sir Peter might agree to an arranged engagement. If he does prefer men and were ever caught out, he would go to prison."

"Do you think that might do the trick?"

"It would certainly save my master's face and would stop a lot of the gossip about her."

"I'll suggest it."

"Then there is charity work. There are soup kitchens in the East End. If she were to work some hours in one of those and the press got to hear of it, she might be regarded as an angel of mercy."

"You are clever, Becket. I wish we could get married."

"We will," said Becket. "I don't know how, but I will do everything in my power to make that happen."

When Daisy returned, Rose listened to Becket's suggestions. "It would mean I would have to propose to Peter," she said.

A footman entered. "Sir Peter Petrey has called, my lady."

"I will see him. Are my parents at home?"

"No, my lady."

"Then put him in the drawing-room. Come, Daisy."

As they walked down to the drawing-room, Daisy hissed, "You can't propose to him with me there."

"We will take tea and then I will ask you to fetch my shawl."

Peter advanced to meet them. "I am so sorry, Lady Rose," he said. "It is unfair that you should be in disgrace for refusing to continue in an engagement that had become distasteful to you. Surely everyone knows he neglected you shamefully."

"Everyone has conveniently forgotten that."

Rose rang the bell and ordered tea. Peter chatted away of this and that and then Rose said, "Please fetch my shawl, Daisy."

When Daisy had left the room, Rose said bluntly, "I have often thought of marrying just anyone in order to have a household of my own."

"You might find a husband tyrannical."

Rose took a deep breath. "Not if it were someone like you."

Peter carefully replaced a half-eaten crumpet on his plate. "Lady Rose, are you proposing to me?"

"I suppose I am. I shall be very rich on my majority. I would not interfere with you if you would not interfere with me."

"Meaning a marriage in name only?"

"Yes."

"Why this sudden desire to marry me and not someone else?"

"I do not like anyone else. If I were to announce an engagement to you, people would assume that was the reason I jilted the captain."

"All very Byzantine. Yes, I don't see why not. We are friends. Ah, I hear your parents returning. I shall ask you father's permission."

Lady Polly was in a high good humour. Ever since Rose's disgrace, she had been diligently making calls, reminding society how Cathcart had snubbed her poor Rose, how he had never been at her side; how, having sunk to trade, the captain spent all his time working like a common labourer. Her last call had shown her that the gossip had taken. "Poor Lady Rose," fickle society was now saying. "Of course she could not go on."

The earl, who had just returned from his club, was told by Brum, "Sir Peter Petrey wishes to speak to you, my lord."

"Does he now!" Lady Polly and her husband exchanged glances.

When they entered the drawing-room, Peter rose to meet them. "My lord, my lady, I will get directly to the point of my call. I wish to marry your daughter."

"You have my permission," sighed the earl. "I'll send Rose to you, but don't get your hopes up."

"Lady Rose has already intimated that she would be pleased to accept my suit."

"Splendid! Splendid!" said the earl. "Leave you to it."

Harry was so furious when he read the announcement that Becket did not dare tell him it had been his idea.

Instead Becket said cautiously, "I fear, sir, that Lady Rose may have been anxious to set up her own household and found in Sir Peter someone amiable who would let her have her own way."

"Oh, to hell with her," raged Harry. "I'm well out of it. I'm going to see Kerridge."

At Scotland Yard, Kerridge looked sympathetically at Harry. "It's your own fault," he said. "You did neglect her."

Harry shrugged. "I may as well tell you now. It was an arrangement between us to stop her being sent out to India."

"That's a pity. I always thought the pair of you were eminently suitable. Still, that's an end to her detecting. She won't be getting into any more trouble now."

In the following weeks Rose began to relax and feel she had made a wise decision. Peter was always in attendance and was a free and easy companion. But there was still some black little piece of sorrow inside her. She told herself it was because she missed the excitement of being with Harry and Becket and solving cases.

One morning, she remembered guiltily that it had been some days since she had last visited Miss Friendly. She went up to the attic. She stopped outside the door. Miss Friendly was singing in a high reedy voice:

> "Under a spreading chestnut-tree
> _ The village smithy stands;
> The smith, a mighty man is he,
> With large and sinewy hands;

And the muscles of his brawny arms
Are strong as iron bands."

Rose pushed open the door and went in. "I heard you singing. I assume that means you are still happy with us, Miss Friendly?"

"So very happy, Lady Rose. Funnily enough, I was just remembering when Roger, the blacksmith's son, used to sing that song. It was originally a Longfellow poem. He had such a lovely voice."

"I wish I knew where this Roger is now," said Rose. "What are you working at?"

Miss Friendly flushed slightly. "I regret to say that I am working for myself just now. I have put on weight and I am letting out a gown."

Rose laughed. "You needed to put on weight." Then she said, "Did you ever do any charity work?"

"When Papa was alive I used to call on the unfortunate of the village. There were so many. I would give them what food we could spare."

"Miss Levine has suggested that I might do some work in the soup kitchens of the East End. Perhaps you might care to accompany me?"

"Gladly. Charity work is very rewarding."

"Then I shall let you know when we are setting out."

Rose went back down the stairs and told Daisy they would be taking Miss Friendly with them when they set out on charity work. To Daisy, a trip to the East End of London was a journey back into her past that she was reluctant to make.

She asked, "Did Miss Friendly remember anything more about Dolly that might be important?"

"No, she was just saying, however, that this Roger Dallow had an excellent singing voice."

Daisy's green eyes gleamed. "If I were a blacksmith's lad and had a good voice and had endured enough hard labour to last me a lifetime, I'd try to get a job in the music hall."

"I never thought of that. But there are so many theatres in London."

"I could go out and buy a copy of *The Stage Directory*. The offices are in Covent Garden opposite the Theatre Royal."

"And you think he might be in there?"

"Perhaps."

"Good. Let us go now. I do not have an engagement until this evening."

They took one of the earl's carriages to Covent Garden. Rose waited until Daisy went in and bought a copy of the paper. She emerged pleased with herself. "It only costs a penny now."

"Let's go to Swan and Edgar for tea. We can look at it there and quiz the ladies' hats."

The department store of Swan and Edgar at Piccadilly Circus was famous for its teas. They also had an orchestra to entertain the customers.

"Now," said Daisy, "let's see if he's in here."

Rose leaned back in her chair and listened to the sugary strains of the orchestra playing "Poor Wandering One" from *The Pirates of Penzance*. Did Harry ever think of her? she wondered.

"There's something here," said Daisy. "It doesn't say Roger Dallow, but it says there's someone called Sam Duval and he's billed at the Fulham Palace Music Hall as The Singing Blacksmith."

"I wish we could go this evening but we are invited to the Pocingtons for dinner."

"You could have a headache."

Rose smiled. "So I could. My parents are so pleased with my engagement that they will not mind me having one night off. The minute they leave, we can take a hansom to Fulham Palace."

Daisy was excited. If they found out anything, surely Rose would want to tell Harry and Kerridge.

When they climbed into the hansom that evening, Daisy twisted around and peered out of the back window.

"What's the matter?" asked Rose.

"Funny," said Daisy, turning back. "I thought I saw two men standing under the trees opposite the house."

"That is odd. Some time ago I looked down into the square and saw Cyril Banks and Lord Berrow standing there."

"I wish you were still engaged to the captain," fretted Daisy. "He would have come round and lain in wait for them and demanded to know what they were doing."

"I'm sure Sir Peter will do the same thing should I ask him."

"He's not frightening enough," said Daisy. "The captain is."

"Oh, do stop talking about Captain Cathcart. That part of my life is finished."

"So you say," muttered Daisy sulkily.

———

They had to pay for a box at the Fulham Palace Music Hall as all the seats had already been booked.

There was to be a guest appearance of George Chevalier, famous for his song "My Old Dutch."

Rose fidgeted restlessly while Daisy heaved a sentimental sigh as Chevalier sang:

"We've been together now for forty years,
An' it don't seem a day too much;
There ain't a lady livin' in the land
As I'd swop for my dear old Dutch."

Then came the comedians, the jugglers, and a conjurer, all followed by a massive corseted lady who sang, "I Dreamt that I Dwelt in Marble Halls." The first half was over.

Rose saw various members of the audience staring up at the box and lowered her veil. But to Daisy, who had been on the halls herself, it was all fascinating.

The second half opened with a man with his performing dogs. Rose stifled a yawn. And then Sam Duval came on. He was an exceptionally good-looking man with dark curly hair and a strong figure. He was dressed in a blacksmith's costume and standing by a "forge" and looking at an empty birdcage on a table in front of the footlights. He sang in a clear tenor voice:

"She's only a bird
In a gilded cage,
A beautiful sight to see,
You may think she's happy
And free from care,
She's not
Tho' she seems to be.

> 'Tis sad when you think
> Of her wasted life,
> For youth cannot mate with age,
> And her beauty was sold
> For an old man's gold,
> She's a bird in a gilded cage."

There was a throb in his voice while he sang. There was a brief silence when he finished and then there was a roar of applause. Daisy clapped until her hands were sore. Then she nudged Rose. "Come on. I'm sure that's him. Let's get round to the stage door."

Frost glittered on the pavement outside the theatre, shining under the stuttering gaslights, as they made their way round to the side of the building.

Rose presented her card to the stage-door keeper. "Follow me," he said, and winked at her. Oh dear, thought Rose. He thinks I'm the female equivalent of a stage-door Johnny.

They followed the stage-door keeper up narrow stairs and along a passage. "That's him," he said, jerking his hand at a door. He turned and left them.

"Here we go," said Daisy. She rapped at the door and a voice called, "Come in."

They entered a small dressing-room which smelled strongly of dog. The Singing Blacksmith was sitting in front of a mirror.

He stared in the mirror at them. "Who are you?"

Rose stepped forward. "I am Lady Rose Summer and this is Mrs. Levine. Are you really Roger Dallow?"

"So what's it to you?"

"I was briefly a friend of Miss Dolly Tremaine. I am trying to find out what happened to her."

He swung round. "I remember your name now. It was in the newspapers."

"Was Miss Tremaine going to join you?"

"Yes. I stood outside the house and she dropped a note out of the window. She said she would join me. She said she couldn't bear it any longer because they were forcing her to marry some old man. She said I was to meet her the following day at the Shaftsbury Monument in Piccadilly at four in the afternoon. The following day, I waited and waited, but she didn't come. Then I heard the newsboys calling out about some murder. I bought a paper. I can't read very well but enough to know she had been murdered."

"Did she ever tell you she was frightened of anyone?" asked Rose.

"I wasn't allowed to go near her in the village after someone reported we'd been seen together. I got a whipping from my dad. I wouldn't have run away but then I heard Dolly had been taken off to London. I don't earn much here but it would have been enough for us to live simply." He buried his head in his hands. "I loved her."

"The police have been looking for you," said Rose. "May I tell them we found you?"

"No!" he cried. "I'd nothing to do with it, but if the police come round here and take me away for questioning, innocent or not, I won't have a job when I get back."

"What's the awful smell in here?" asked Daisy, wrinkling her nose.

"I've got to share with the dog act. He's taken them out for a walk."

"So you have no idea at all who might have killed her?" asked Rose.

"Who would want to kill Dolly except that Lord Berrow? Maybe he got mad when she told him she wouldn't marry him."

"I do not think she would be allowed to do anything other than accept his proposal," said Rose.

"Someone tried to kill you, didn't they?" asked Roger.

"Yes, the police now think it was some hired assassin. I will not tell the police about you."

The dressing-room door opened and a pretty chorus girl came in. "Nearly time for the curtain call, darling." She perched on Roger's knee and gave him a hearty kiss. Roger threw a sheepish look at Rose.

"Who're they?" asked the chorus girl.

"Nobody, really," said Roger.

Rose and Daisy left.

"So much for undying love," said Rose. "He seems to have found someone new pretty quickly."

"It's been months since the murder," said the ever-pragmatic Daisy. "Life goes on."

Rose brooded on Harry on the journey back. She had never thought until that moment that Harry might fall in love and get married. The idea depressed her.

Daisy broke into her thoughts. "Going to tell the captain about Roger?"

"No."

"He might have done it."

"He hasn't enough money to pay an assassin. Don't tell Becket anything."

"Cross my heart and hope to die."

Harry had been visiting a house a few doors away from the earl's town house to report that he had managed to quash a scandal.

As he left, he suddenly stopped on the front stairs. Two men were looking up at the earl's house. When they saw Harry, they moved away.

Berrow and Banks, thought Harry. Why are they spying on Rose? I don't like this at all.

They were walking away quickly, but he caught up with them. "Stop!" he shouted. "What were you doing watching Hadfield's house?"

Cyril stared at him insolently. "We stopped to have a cigar."

"You were not smoking."

"See here," said Berrow, shoving his fat and florid face at Harry, "you're a cheeky upstart. You've betrayed your class. How dare you question me!"

"I'm warning you," said Harry, "if I catch you here again, I'll beat the living daylights out of you, and if either of you had anything to do with the murder of Dolly Tremaine, I'll find out."

They backed away from him, turned, and walked rapidly out of the square.

"Needs to be taught a lesson," growled Berrow. "Have you seen that motor of his? He's making a fortune out of his grubby business. I'd like to punish him. Are you sure Lady Rose really fancies you? I mean, she got engaged to Petrey."

"And we all know what Petrey is. I tell you, Lady Rose was all over me. Think of her fortune. Think of getting the Ice Queen into bed. But I've got to get rid of Petrey and I've thought of a way."

Sir Peter Petrey was leaving The Club two days later. London was in the grip of a particularly nasty thick yellow fog. It was one of those lung-searing fogs of winter blanketing London, blotting out landmarks. He knew if he could even get a hansom, it would take him ages to get home.

It was late afternoon and he realized he would need to walk home if he was to manage to change into his evening clothes and escort Rose to a dinner party.

He bumped into someone in the fog. "I say, I am sorry," he said.

"It's all right. Beastly weather," said a young voice. "Do you know the way to Charles Street?"

"I'm going there myself. Come along."

They walked on together. As they passed a lighted shop front, the fog swirled for a moment and thinned. Peter looked at his companion and caught his breath. He was looking at the face of an angel. Golden hair like guineas glinted under a silk hat, large deep eyes, a perfect skin, and a mouth like Cupid's bow.

"Are you visiting London?" he asked.

"No, I live here. I'm going to visit friends. This is awfully good of you, sir."

"My name is Peter Petrey. And you are . . . ?"

"Jonathan Wilks."

"I am glad of the company on such a filthy night, Mr. Wilks."

"Do call me Jonathan, everyone does."

They talked about plays they had seen and poetry they had read. Peter began not to notice the fog. He felt he was enclosed in a golden bubble with this dazzling youth.

Just before they reached Peter's house, the young man stopped. "This is where I leave you."

"Here is my card," said Peter. "Do call. I'll wait to see you get in safely."

Jonathan knocked at the door. Then he came back down the front steps. "They don't seem to be at home. I must have forgotten the day. This is Friday, is it not?"

"No, it's Thursday."

"Oh dear."

"Look, come in with me and have a sherry while I dress."

When Peter arrived slightly late and out of breath, Rose noticed he seemed to shine with an inner glow. Oh dear, she thought, I hope I haven't made a mistake about him. He looks like a man in love.

Peter had never been in better form than during the dinner. He told jokes, he told gossip, and he delighted the company.

Shrewd Daisy watched him with anxious eyes. I hope it's Rose that has given him this extra sparkle, she thought. I hope it isn't anyone it shouldn't be.

Daisy's concerns grew when, after dinner, she heard Peter tell Rose that he was going away on Friday and would not return until the following Monday.

"Where?" asked Rose. "Anywhere pleasant?"

"Just visiting some friends."

"You will miss the ball tomorrow."

"Oh dear. Can you find someone to escort you? Captain Cathcart, perhaps?"

Rose raised her brows in amazement. "Have you forgotten I ended my engagement to the captain and became engaged to you?"

"No, my dearest. It is just that it is very important that I go away this weekend."

126

"What is so important?"

Peter manufactured a laugh. "You sound like a wife already. Ah, there is Lady Simpson looking for me."

He darted off.

Daisy joined Rose. "I heard that."

"Most odd," said Rose. "Just a day ago he seemed to delight in my company."

"Let's just hope he isn't delighting in anyone else's."

Peter and Jonathan went down to Oxford the following day. The fog had disappeared, but Oxford was shrouded in a hard frost. They walked along by the icy river where the last leaves hung rimed with the frost, which glinted like rubies under a hard red sun. Peter kept glancing at his companion, becoming even more and more besotted. Those large eyes that he had first seen in the fog were green with flecks of gold. His black eyelashes were thick and curled at the ends. He had a wide-brimmed hat perched rakishly on his golden curls.

Peter considered him too perfect for any carnal thoughts. His sexual adventures had been very few and he had avoided that brothel in Westminster which catered to tastes like his own. Discretion was all-important. Discovery meant prison and hard labour.

They had a pleasant dinner that evening at the Rose and Crown. When they had finished, Peter dabbed his mouth with his napkin. "Now what shall we do?"

Jonathan leaned forward and fixed him with a glowing look. "I know somewhere in Oxford where we can end the evening . . . together. It's not much of a hotel, but it would serve our purpose."

Peter's mouth went dry. "Y-you c-can't mean . . ." he stuttered. That beautiful mouth smiled at him lazily.

"Oh, but that's exactly what I mean."

Rose sat at the ball and watched the dancers. Now that she was engaged to Peter and seemed happy with him, the heiress-hunters of society had decided to leave her alone.

The next dance, a waltz, was announced. She looked at her dance card. Nothing for the next dance and then a few dances with elderly friends of her father.

She looked up and found Harry bowing before her. "Lady Rose, may I have the honour?"

They moved together on the dance floor. "Have you any more news about Dolly's death?" asked Rose.

"Nothing, I'm afraid. Have you?"

Rose thought of Roger but decided to remain silent. She shook her head.

"Where is your fiancé tonight?"

"He has gone off to see friends."

"That is surely most unlike him. I would have thought him a dutiful escort."

"He usually is."

"Are you sure you want to go through with this marriage? Don't you want children?"

"I do not know what you mean."

"Daisy told me that you know exactly what I mean. Peter is not interested in your sex."

"There is no proof of that," said Rose, her face flaming. "In any case, all I want is an arranged marriage. I would have my own household and I would have freedom. I owe you an apology. I only found out later that you had been the hero of that terrible train crash."

"On another matter, I found Berrow and Banks outside your house. I warned them off. What are they up to?"

"I don't know."

"While we had our pretend engagement, at least I could feel I was protecting you."

"Fiddlesticks. You were never there."

"I could change," he muttered.

"What did you say?" demanded Rose, but the waltz had finished and an elderly partner was waiting for her.

She danced impatiently, wanting to speak to Harry again, wondering if he had really said he could change, and what had he meant by that?

When the dance was over, her eyes searched the ballroom, but there was no sign of Harry.

Peter and Jonathan lay side by side, naked, on a bed in a seedy hotel in Oxford's Jericho district. Jonathan was smoking a Russian cigarette and blowing smoke rings up to the ceiling.

"That was beautiful," said Peter in a choked voice.

"I can make it more exciting." Jonathan stubbed out his cigarette and then fished on the floor on his side of the bed. He brought up a leather mask. "If I put this on, it will titillate you even more."

"I am in love with you," said Peter in a stifled voice. "I do not need to play silly games."

"You'll love it. See!" Jonathan put the mask on and then wound his arms around Peter. "Indulge me." Then he raised his voice. "I have the mask on!"

The bedroom door burst open and a magnesium flash blinded Peter. The man behind the flash was holding a camera. He, too, was masked. The cameraman snapped at Jonathan, "You've done your work. Now get out of here."

Jonathan scooped up his clothes and darted from the room. Peter struggled out of bed and ran to the door, which was slammed in his face. He hurriedly dressed and ran downstairs and into the street.

He looked frantically up and down. No one. He went back to the hotel. "Who was that man with the camera?" he demanded.

The man at reception looked at him with flat eyes. "I never saw nobody with a camera."

"You're lying," howled Peter.

The man smiled at him. "Want to go to the police?"

"That is what I am going to do," said Peter, knowing miserably that that was the very last thing he could do.

He could only assume that whoever took that photo meant to blackmail him. Then he thought of detective Harry Cathcart, who was famous for covering up scandals. But would Harry report him to the police?

It was either that or kill himself.

Harry had gone to visit his father, Baron Derrington, a duty call he had been putting off for ages, and so Peter had to fret and worry all weekend.

When Harry arrived at his office on Monday morning, it was to find Peter waiting for him.

"How can I help you, Sir Peter?" asked Harry.

"May I talk to you in private?" Peter cast a nervous look at the secretary, Ailsa.

"By all means," said Harry. "Come into my office." He cast a shrewd look at the trembling and sweating Peter and said to his secretary, "Miss Bridge, would you please go to Fortnum's and buy me some chocolates? A large box. Take the money out of the petty cash."

"Certainly, sir."

Inside his inner office, Harry held up his hand for silence until he heard Ailsa leaving.

"Now, Sir Peter, you may begin."

"You will despise me!"

"Sir Peter, I know so many shocking things that anything you say will fail to amaze me."

So, in a trembling voice, Peter told him of Jonathan and of how he had been betrayed. He ended by saying, "Do you think they will blackmail me?"

"Probably. Unless—"

The telephone rang. "Excuse me," said Harry. A voice quacked down the receiver from the other end. "I'll be there as soon as I can," said Harry.

"I am afraid," he said to Peter, "that the photograph has gone to Lord Hadfield."

"I am ruined," said Peter, beginning to sob.

"I will make sure Lord Hadfield says nothing of this. But I must get that photograph and negative back."

"But how can you?" wailed Peter. "I don't know who they are."

Harry thought of Berrow and Banks lurking in the square outside Rose's house.

"I want you to go to your home. Speak to no one. Do not answer the door. I will call on you later. I will give three knocks and then two so that you know it is me."

SEVEN
++

> The Governor was strong upon
> The Regulations Act:
> The Doctor said that Death was but
> A scientific fact:
> And twice a day the Chaplain called,
> And left a little tract.
>
> — OSCAR WILDE

Rose wondered what on earth was going on. Her father had put down his newspaper and had stared to look through the morning post. He slit open a square manila envelope. He drew out a photograph. He goggled at it, thrust it back in the envelope and shouted, "Get Cathcart. Now!"

Despite wondering frantically what had been in that photograph, Rose felt a surge of pleasure at the thought she might see Harry again.

"What on earth is going on?" she asked her mother.

"I am sure your father will cope with whatever it is. Eat your breakfast," said Lady Polly.

"Pervert," muttered the earl.

"What did you say?" demanded Rose.

"Hey, what? Oh, I said perishing newspapers."

Rose had never seen her father look so upset. His face was scarlet. At last he said to his wife, "A word with you, dear."

Rose and Daisy picked at their food. Then Rose heard her mother scream.

They ran to the office. The earl shouted at them, "Get out of here! Go to your rooms and don't come out until I tell you."

They went upstairs and stood by the window. At last they saw Harry arriving. Becket was not with him.

"Now what?" asked Rose.

Daisy gave a dismal little shrug. She had been expecting to see Becket.

Harry looked at the photograph. "Nasty," he said. "Sir Peter was entrapped."

"You can't be entrapped unless you're a . . . you're a . . ."

"Quite," said Harry. "Will you leave this with me? I think perhaps I might be able to get the negative and any prints. Petrey will go abroad for an extended period and it will all blow over."

"Rose will need to cancel the engagement!"

"Not yet. I have a feeling that that was just what someone wanted her to do. Leave it to me."

"Usual fee?" asked the earl glumly.

"No, you may have my researches as a present, for it will be my pleasure to deal with whoever did this."

"What do we say to Rose?" asked Lady Polly.

"I think you will find out that your daughter knew of Peter's tastes."

"What?"

"I do not for a moment think she believed that men actually had sexual intercourse—"

"Lady present," growled the earl.

"But that she thought their love was platonic. She craved an arranged marriage."

"Why?"

"Because she does not want to be shipped off to India. If you threaten her with that, she will find someone else."

The earl mopped his brow.

"And I thought you were the worst thing that could have happened to her."

"Thank you for the compliment. Now, leave this with me."

Harry did not go back to his office but returned to Chelsea to ask Becket's advice. He told his manservant about the incriminating photograph. "Do you know anything about the homosexual underworld, Becket?"

"There is that brothel in Westminster that no one is supposed to know about. Who do you suspect, sir?"

"I suspect Berrow and Banks."

"Perhaps they hired a youth from there."

"I am sure a place like that would give me no information whatsoever. I wonder why the police haven't raided the place."

"Possibly there are too many important people who visit there."

"Where exactly is it?"

"Verney Street. I've heard servants gossiping about it."

"I'll go down tonight and watch who comes and goes. I'll visit Petrey first."

———

Harry went to Petrey's home and knocked as arranged. Petrey himself answered the door, looking haggard.

Harry followed him in. He sat down and removed his hat. "The situation is this. Your engagement to Lady Rose stands. You will invent a dying aunt in the south of France. You will write Lady Rose a letter saying you have the leave the country immediately. I think the purpose of your entrapment was to get Lady Rose to break off your engagement. We will not give them that satisfaction right away.

"Now, give me a full description of this Jonathan Wilks."

"He is very beautiful—young, with golden hair and large green eyes with flecks of gold. He is quite tall with a slim body. His skin is clear and without blemish. Believe me, there cannot be very many young men as beautiful as he is in London."

"Leave it to me."

Harry walked to Westminster that evening after the lamps had been lit. To his relief, Verney Street was short. He found a dark doorway and settled down to watch.

At first it was hard to tell which of the dark houses could be a brothel, but then, as the evening drove on, he saw a house in the middle of the street was beginning to be visited by various men who looked nervously up and down before hurrying inside. To his amazement, he recognized a major-general and then a member of Parliament. Still, he waited patiently as the evening dragged on past midnight. There was a cold nip in the air and he wished he had worn a warmer coat. The old wound in his leg was beginning to throb, and as the time approached two in the morning he was just about to give up when he saw a young man emerging from the building.

Before he crammed his hat on his curls, they shone gold in the lamplight.

He started to walk briskly and Harry followed him. The youth went as far as the seedier end of Westminster and turned in at a doorway and disappeared.

Harry went up and lit a match and studied the names beside the bell-pulls.

Jonathan Wilks lived on the top floor. Goodness, thought Harry, he even used his own name.

He took out a set of lock picks and got to work on the outside door until he was able to enter.

He walked silently up the stairs to the top. The name "Wilks" was there, pencilled on the peeling wall beside the door.

Harry knocked. "Who is it?" he heard him call.

Taking a gamble, Harry shouted, "Banks!"

The door swung open. Harry shoved Jonathan backwards into his flat. The young man stumbled and fell on the floor. Harry pulled him up by the lapels and thrust him into an armchair.

"Now," he said, "before I ruin that pretty face of yours for life, you will tell me who paid you to entrap Sir Peter Petrey."

"I don't know what you are talking about."

Harry jerked him out of the chair and drew back his fist.

"No!" screamed Jonathan. "I'll tell you. They said it was just a prank. I was to pretend to bump into him. Then we arranged to go to Oxford, so they said they would book a hotel and gave me the name. They also gave me a leather mask. They said I was to put it on and say in a loud voice something about having the mask on and then they would do the rest."

"And just who are 'they'?"

Jonathan hung his head. "Lord Berrow and Cyril Banks,"

he whispered. Then he began to cry, saying between his sobs, "Don't hurt me."

"You gave me what I wanted. Now, a word of advice. You will forget this ever happened or I will come looking for you. Do I make myself clear?"

"Y-yes."

"I suggest you find yourself a protector and get out of that brothel or you will look like a diseased old man by the time you are thirty. Good night!"

"Wait! Where is Peter?"

"None of your business."

Harry began to walk until he managed to hail a cab and directed the driver to Cyril's address.

Once there, he paid off the cab and waited until the driver had driven off. Then he took out his lock picks and unlocked the front door.

He made his way silently up the thickly carpeted stairs, opening one door after another until he found Cyril's bedroom. He lit the gas and stood and looked down at the sleeping Cyril. He had a sudden impulse to drive his fist into Cyril's face but restrained himself. He looked around the room. There was a laudanum bottle on the bedside table with a spoon beside it. Cyril lay in a drugged sleep.

Harry was sure Cyril would have hidden any negative close to him. There was a safe in the corner, an old one which opened with a key rather than a combination. On a console table lay a bunch of keys. Harry picked them up and tried them until he found the key that opened the safe.

Inside he found a Kodak camera. He peered at the small film window, but saw nothing there. The film had already been removed and the camera was empty. He searched in the safe again and found an envelope with the negative and one print. He stuffed them into his inside coat pocket and locked the safe.

He then walked to Charles Street and gave his special knock at the door. Again Peter answered it. He was fully dressed and his face showed the mark of tears.

"I have a photograph and the negative," said Harry.

"Oh, thank God! Who did this to me?"

"Cyril Banks and Lord Berrow."

"But why? Why me?"

"As I told you in my office, I think the intention was to get Lady Rose to break off your engagement. I suggest you rouse your man and pack. Leave tomorrow. Where will you go?"

"The south of France, where I am supposed to be."

"Stay there a few months and this will all blow over. Hadfield is not going to talk."

"What about Berrow and Banks?"

"You need not fear them. I will deal with them."

Jonathan awoke after an uneasy sleep. He dressed and glanced down at the street. Lord Berrow and Cyril Banks had just turned the corner and were heading in the direction of the house where he lived. Cyril had found the photograph and negative gone and knew that Jonathan must have talked.

Jonathan let out a squawk of terror.

The doorbell jangled furiously. Jonathan began to pack a bag. He kept glancing fearfully out of the window until he saw them walk away.

He darted down the stairs, carrying his bag, and called a cab. "Charles Street," he said.

Peter walked out to his carriage. It was later in the morning than he had intended to leave, but sheer relief had made him fall into a deep sleep. The carriage was loaded with his luggage.

He had one foot on the step when he heard a voice shout, "Peter! Wait!"

Peter stared as Jonathan hurtled towards him.

"You little bastard," hissed Peter. He started to climb into the carriage.

"They told me it was only a prank," said Jonathan, tears running down his face. "They are going to kill me. Take me with you."

"I am going to the south of France to forget about the whole sordid business."

Peter climbed into the carriage and rapped on the roof with his cane. The carriage lurched forward. Jonathan jumped on the backstrap.

Twisting round, Peter saw the youth's anguished face through the back window.

He turned away in disgust.

When the hansom stopped in the forecourt of Charing Cross Station, where Peter was booked on the Dover train, he told his manservant, "Get a porter. Now, you," he said, glaring at Jonathan, "run along."

"Take me with you. I'll do anything. I hate the life here. Please."

In his anger and distress, Peter could not help noticing that tears did not mar or blotch the beauty of that face. He decided to pretend that Jonathan did not exist.

He heaved a sigh of relief when he was finally settled by

his manservant in a first-class compartment. "Take care of the house when I am gone," said Peter.

Just as the train began to move forwards out of the station, the carriage door opened and Jonathan tumbled in.

"What am I to do?" demanded the furious Peter. "I cannot call the guard in case you shame me further."

"I thought it was a joke. I never expected to like you so much. I'm frightened," said Jonathan.

Peter raised a newspaper and pretended to read. After several miles, the quiet sobbing opposite melted him a little.

"Luncheon is served," called a waiter.

Peter sighed and lowered the newspaper. "Dry your eyes. We may as well eat."

Rose wondered what on earth was going on. "If only we could get to the captain's office," she said to Daisy.

"We could simply say we were going for a walk," said Daisy.

"At the moment we are not allowed out of the house."

"I'll watch by the window and see whether my lord and my lady go out. My lord goes to his club most days." Daisy took up a position by the window.

After quarter of an hour, she said, "There he goes. Now we need to wait for Lady Polly."

The day dragged on. Rose read while Daisy kept watch. "Lady Polly has just left," she exclaimed.

Rose put down her book. "How do we get past the servants?"

"They'll be taking afternoon tea," said Daisy. "If we hurry, we should get out unnoticed."

"What about coming back?"

"Let's worry about that later. We'll go to Chelsea. He may have finished work by the time we get there."

At Harry's Chelsea home, Daisy bit back an exclamation of disappointment as Phil opened the door to them.

"Is Captain Cathcart at home?" asked Rose.

"I am expecting him at any moment."

Rose handed him her card. "We will wait."

"Certainly, my lady. Step this way. Sherry, my lady?"

"Yes, please."

"Who on earth is that?" hissed Daisy when Phil had left the room.

"I believe he is some down-and-out that the captain rescued from poverty."

Phil returned carrying sherry glasses and a decanter on a tray. He carefully poured two glasses and handed one to Rose and then one to Daisy.

He bowed low. "Will there be h'anythink else, my lady?"

"No, I thank you."

Phil bowed his way out of the room.

Daisy looked around the book-lined parlour. "You would think with all the money he's making he would find a more fashionable address."

"Shh! I hear a motor car."

Harry walked in, followed by Becket. "Lady Rose! What brings you here?"

"I must know what is going on," said Rose. "What was in that photograph?"

Becket helped Harry out of his coat and took his hat and stick. He smiled at Daisy, who gave him a cheeky wink.

Harry sat down. "The photograph was of Sir Peter in a

compromising position with a beautiful youth wearing a mask."

"You can't mean . . . Gentlemen don't . . ."

"I am afraid they do. Berrow and Banks paid the young man to entrap Sir Peter."

"Have you been to Kerridge? You must tell the police."

"I cannot tell the police. Kerridge would be honour-bound to arrest Sir Peter. He would be charged with acts of gross indecency and sentenced to hard labour."

Rose's face was bright red. "I never imagined . . . I never thought . . . Where is Peter?"

"Well on his way to the south of France, I hope."

Rose stared at him for a long moment. "Do you see what this means? If Berrow and Banks hired this youth to compromise Sir Peter, then they are probably the ones who hired the assassin to try to kill me."

"That is possible. Although I fear one of them wanted Petrey out of the way so that he could try his luck with you. But I definitely cannot tell Kerridge. I am going out this evening to silence Berrow and Banks."

"You will kill them?"

"No, my dear. There are other ways."

"I cannot understand why my father did not cancel my engagement."

"He will. But I did not, for the moment, want Berrow or Banks to have that satisfaction. Now I need to go out again. May Becket take you home?"

"Yes, please."

Harry rang the bell. "Becket, take Miss Levine out to the motor. I need a word with Lady Rose in private."

When they had left, Harry looked seriously at Rose. "I am

going to ask your father's permission to pay my addresses to you. What do you think of that?"

"He will never agree. And why?"

He wanted to say, Because you enchant and infuriate me. Instead he said, "Because I would not leave you unprotected. London is full of adventurers. You may make another mistake."

"But you will leave me alone like you did before!"

"I will try to behave like a faithful swain. Come, Rose, we are both misfits and we could deal well together."

Rose looked up at him from beneath her long lashes. "An arrangement like before?"

"If you wish."

At last she gave a little sigh. "Very well, then."

"I must deal with Berrow and Banks first. Then I will call."

"I am only agreeing because at the moment I am not allowed out of the house."

Harry smiled. "Let me escort you out to the motor."

Harry waited until Becket had returned. "Do not take off your coat, Becket. We are going to Scotland Yard. How is Phil progressing with the camera work?"

"He is excellent and knows how to develop and print negatives."

"Good. Tell him to get that new Kodak I bought him, film, and magnesium for the flash. I'll need him tonight. I will also need to furnish you with a pistol, Becket. You do not mind threatening anyone with a pistol, do you?"

"Certainly not, sir."

"So here's what we will do . . ."

Harry hoped his guess was correct—that Berrow and Banks would wait outside that brothel in the hope of getting hold of Jonathan. But to make sure, he, Becket, and Phil followed the pair from The Club, then hid at the end of Verney Street and watched. Berrow and Banks looked around furtively and went into the brothel. They came out a few minutes later and stood waiting.

"Jonathan must have been due on duty about now," whispered Harry. "Becket and Phil, go now. You have your instructions."

Becket walked forward to where Berrow and Cyril were standing. Harry had altered his manservant's appearance. Becket now sported a heavy moustache and mutton-chop whiskers.

He held the gun on the pair. Then he raised it and fired a shot neatly through the top of Berrow's silk hat and then levelled the pistol on them again.

The brothel door slammed shut and the lights went out. A shot in Verney Street meant trouble, and trouble meant the police. No one wanted to be around when the police arrived. Harry at the end of the street saw a possible customer turn and run off.

"What do you want?" squeaked Cyril. "Our money?"

"I want you to kiss your friend on the mouth."

"Bugger you," hissed Berrow.

Becket clicked back the hammer on the pistol. "Oh, do what the maniac says," howled Cyril, "or he'll kill us."

He grasped Berrow by the shoulders and pressed his mouth to his. Becket melted into the shadows as the magnesium flare went off.

Neither man saw the flash, both having their eyes tight

shut. When Cyril released Berrow, he looked wildly around. There was no sign of anyone. Both men took out their silk handkerchiefs and wiped their mouths.

"Disgusting!" raged Berrow. "Let's get out of here. Scotland Yard shall hear of this." He set off down the street.

"Hold on," said Cyril. "We can't tell the police."

"Why not? We were forced to kiss each other by some maniac with a pistol."

"The police will ask where it took place. If we say Verney Street, they'll think we're a pair of you-know-whats. And I told you that someone opened my safe and stole that negative and photograph."

Berrow stopped short. "What are we to do?"

"We can't do anything."

The next morning, both Cyril and Berrow received envelopes delivered by hand. In each envelope was a large photograph of them kissing each other. The brothel behind them was also in the picture. Each received the same letter. "If you go near Lady Rose Summer again or interfere in her life, go near her home, or threaten her in any way, this photograph goes to the police and the newspapers."

Cyril went straight round to Berrow's town house.

"You got one too! What are we to do?"

"I'm sure this is the work of that counter-jumper, Cathcart," growled Berrow. "Let's keep clear of Lady Rose while we think of a way to get back at him."

The earl was having a late breakfast with his wife when he was told that Captain Cathcart had called.

"Send him in," he ordered, and when Harry arrived, "have some breakfast. Pull up a pew."

"Just coffee, please," said Harry. A cup of coffee was given to him by a footman.

"Have you any news?"

"Not before the servants," said Harry.

"You lot, get out of here," ordered the earl. "And no listening at the door, either." He turned to his wife. "You'd better go, too, my dear. Unsavoury stuff."

"Before you go, Lady Polly, and before I give my report, I wish to inform you that I would consider it a great honour to renew my engagement to your daughter."

"Not that again," said the earl.

"I think you will find that your daughter is not indifferent to my suit. Lady Rose needs someone to protect her from danger."

"You drag her into danger!"

"I had nothing to do with her finding that body in Hyde Park."

"True. Oh, well, after your behaviour the last time you were engaged to her, she won't want anything to do with you. Try if you like. Now, to business. My dear?"

When Lady Polly had left the room, Harry described how Berrow and Cyril had been forced to kiss each other. "They know that should they even go near Lady Rose again, the photograph will be sent to the police and to the newspapers."

The earl began to laugh. Rose had seen Harry arrive. She could hear her father's roars of laughter and wondered if it could be because Harry had asked for her hand in marriage once more.

"By Jove," said the earl, "that's brilliant. But why don't the police shut that den of iniquity down?"

"I am afraid high-ranking people use it."

"Demme, this town's a sewer, a veritable sewer. Ghastly fellows preferring it up the tradesmen's entrance. Thanks anyway. I suppose you'd better see Rose, but mark my words, you're in for a rough rejection."

The earl and countess were bemused when they were asked to come to the drawing-room to find their daughter wearing a sparkling engagement ring and smiling up at the captain.

"Your daughter has done me the great honour of accepting my hand in marriage," said Harry.

"I think you're both mad," roared the earl and stormed from the room. Lady Polly remained. "I suppose Mr. Jarvis will have to cancel your engagement now to Sir Peter and then announce this engagement. Really, Rose, do try in future to be more *conventional*. Brum said he saw you sneaking back into the house when I had given you strict instructions not to leave it. You may take your leave, Captain Cathcart. Mr. Jarvis will let you know of Rose's social engagements."

Harry kissed Rose on her cheek. "Friends again?" he whispered.

"Friends," echoed Rose softly.

To Rose's relief, her mother made no protest at her plan to help the poor of East London by serving in the soup kitchen at St. Matthew's in Whitechapel. Charity was fashionable provided one went armoured with the usual protection of footman and lady's maid.

Rose decided to take Miss Friendly with her, Daisy having suddenly and vehemently refused to go.

Daisy said she didn't want to run into old acquaintances. It wasn't because she had become too grand, it was because they'd make a mock of her while demanding money at the same time.

So Rose set off the following morning, Matthew having arranged her visit with the vicar.

The lady running the soup kitchen was a Mrs. Harrison, whom Rose remembered from her suffragette meetings. She was a thickset middle-class woman with a no-nonsense air.

She supplied Rose and Miss Friendly with long aprons to protect their clothes and told them to supply their own next time.

Rose had not been prepared for the rank smell of so many diseased and unwashed bodies. But she smiled and ladled soup into bowls while Miss Friendly handed out chunks of bread.

Her beauty was appreciated by the poor. She smiled at each and said a few words of comfort. One old Cockney was particularly grateful. "The Good Lord sent you, missus," he said. "I saw the light in prison, I did. Chaplain says God would take care of me. You is an instrument of the Lord."

He moved on. Rose's feet began to ache. "How long do we have to stay here?" she whispered to Miss Friendly.

"Another hour," murmured Miss Friendly. "So many hungry people."

At last it was over. Rose felt a glow of achievement as she was driven off. She had promised to return on the following day.

Her scalp became increasingly itchy as the day wore on. She rang for her lady's maid. "Turner, would you see if I have a rash on my scalp?"

Turner took the bone pins and pads out of Rose's elaborate hair-style and brushed out her long hair.

"My lady, you have lice!"

"Lice!"

"Head lice. I will fetch a tooth comb and disinfectant."

Rose spent an agonizing hour bent over a sheet of white paper while Turner combed out the lice with a toothcomb soaked in disinfectant. Then her hair was washed several times.

Rose remembered that Mrs. Harrison's hair had been bound up in a tight turban. She could only be glad that she was free of social engagements that evening. What if all the lice had not been discovered and some fell on the captain!

When she went to sleep that night, she dreamt she was floating down the river in the rowing-boat with Dolly. "You've missed something. It's right under your nose," said Dolly. Rose awoke with a start. Someone had said something or done something recently that was important. She racked her brain, but could not think what it was.

EIGHT

✥

A man cannot be too careful in the choice of his enemies.

—OSCAR WILDE

Harry visited Kerridge the next day. "Did you ever interview Lord Berrow?" he asked.

"Yes, but got nothing but the usual bluster out of him."

"He is a nasty, brutal man. Maybe he knew Dolly was going to run away. I really feel you should interview him again. I'll come with you. He'll still be at his town house."

"I'll try anything. I don't like unfinished cases, particularly murder ones."

Accompanied by Inspector Judd, they went to Lord Berrow's home. When Berrow heard that a detective superintendent from Scotland Yard had called, he could almost feel his heart shrivel into a tiny knot of panic.

"Very well. I will see this person," he told his butler loftily. "Put him in the library. Has he come alone?"

"There is a police inspector with him and a Captain Cathcart."

Berrow wondered whether to make a run for it out of the back door or bluster it out. Bluster won.

He entered the library with a breezy, "What ho! One of my servants been stealing the silver?"

"I have neglected to ask you, my lord, what you were doing on the evening that Miss Tremaine was murdered."

Relief flooded Lord Berrow's corpulent body. "Get out of here. You are insolent. Do you know who I am?"

"Answer the question," said Harry in a level voice.

Berrow stared at him for a long moment. He was sure it was Cathcart who was behind the taking of that dreadful photograph.

To Kerridge's amazement, Berrow said mildly, "Sorry. But you caught me on the hop. Let me see. It's a while back. I was at The Club. You can ask the other members. I stayed there until two in the morning. Went home, went to bed. That's it."

"You do not have any connection with criminals, do you?" asked Kerridge, thinking that if Berrow had hired an assassin, it didn't really matter what sort of alibi he had.

"My dear fellow, I do not know such types. I consort with the highest in the land, including our King."

Kerridge fixed a flat-eyed gaze on him. Berrow shifted uneasily, not knowing that Kerridge was dreaming of him being shot by a firing squad at the people's revolution, masterminded by himself. He could see this fat lord trembling as he shouted, "Fire!" Then he realized to his consternation that he had shouted aloud.

"What fire? Where?" Berrow looked wildly around. "I don't have electricity." People in homes lit by electricity often sat with cushions at the ready to throw at the skirting as the occasional over-powerful surge of electricity caused it to burst into flames.

"My apologies. I was thinking of something else."

They questioned him further, Berrow growing more and more relaxed when he realized there was to be no mention of that photograph.

But when they had left, he phoned Cyril to tell him of the visit. "I can't take any more frights like this morning," he said. "We've got to get that negative."

"He might keep it at his office. I've heard there's only a secretary there."

"We'll watch his office."

"He might see us. I'll send a servant to let us know. We'll wait in a coffee shop nearby."

Ailsa Bridge, Harry secretary, was not her usual placid self because she had run out of gin. While she knew her employer kept drinks in his inner office, she dismissed the idea. That would be stealing. But she began to make mistakes in her typing. She looked longingly at the door of the inner office, where the bottles in the cupboard seemed to be singing a siren song to her.

It was too much. She got to her feet. The telephone rang, making her jump guiltily. It was Harry. "I won't be back for a couple of hours," he said. "I don't have any appointments, do I?"

"Three o'clock is the next one," said Ailsa.

"Good. I can trust you as usual to take care of anything that arises."

Ailsa replaced the receiver and stood, lost in thought. If she went out to buy gin, he wouldn't know. But what if some important case came up and she wasn't there?

"Just a little fortifier," she murmured and headed for the

inner office. She crouched down by the cupboard. "Whisky, brandy, sherry, but no gin. Blast!"

Whisky would have to do. She extracted the cork with her teeth and took a large swig, feeling the spirit coursing through her veins. And then she heard footsteps on the stairs. She rammed the cork back in the bottle when she heard a man's voice say, "The place is empty. Let's get to work before the bastard gets back."

Ailsa, the prim, spinsterish daughter of missionaries, had been in a lot of difficult situations in Burma. She carefully took the revolver Harry kept in his desk and, holding it behind her thin figure, emerged from the inner office.

Two masked men stood there. The heavy-set one advanced on her. "Sit down and keep your mouth shut," he growled, "or it will be the worse for you."

Ailsa produced the revolver from behind her back. "Get out," she said calmly.

They both stopped short. The other man gave a sniggering laugh. "A little lady like you shouldn't be playing with guns."

Ailsa levelled the gun and shot him in the foot. He screamed and fell down. Ailsa picked up the receiver and said, "Police."

"Let's get out of here!" screamed the injured one. "I'm dying!"

Helped by his companion, they both stumbled out of the office and down the stairs.

The injured party was Cyril Banks and he had to wait, moaning and crying, while Berrow found a doctor who would keep his mouth shut, knowing that the police would be checking the hospitals. Because he was an inveterate smoker and kept a spare cigarette case inside his elastic-sided boot, his foot was only badly bruised.

After the doctor had left, he and Berrow sat down to think up ways and means of getting that photograph back.

Harry knew who the culprits probably were and told the police. But when they called on Cyril, it was to find he appeared to be walking normally and there was no sign he had been shot. Threatened with everyone from the king to the prime minister, the police backed off with apologies.

When he heard the news, Harry assumed that they had hired a couple of men. "Maybe," he said to Ailsa, "you should take some leave. They will try again."

"I am not afraid," said Ailsa, "although I did have a fright. I am afraid I helped myself to some of your whisky."

"That's all right. But be vigilant. There is a police guard now on the door downstairs."

"We need to be subtle," said Berrow. "She looked like a real dried-up spinster. What about getting someone to romance her? Let me think. Who needs money?"

"Most of London society."

"We need a charming wastrel."

"There's Guy Delancey. Still owes me a packet from a baccarat game. But if he courts her and gets that negative, maybe there's another print with it and he'll see that photograph."

"Don't worry. I'll tell him how we were set up."

The dark days moved on to Christmas. The earl was preparing to remove to Stacey Court in the country. Harry had been invited to join them, and to Rose's amazement had accepted. He had been at her side as much as he could, but always at social occasions, and had not seemed to make any push to be alone with her.

Rose still diligently worked at the soup kitchen, forgetting in her zeal that the idea had originally been to get her photograph in the newspapers. She now wore her hair tightly bound up in a disinfected turban. At times she wearied of the smell and degradation of the people she was serving and could only marvel at Miss Friendly's unremitting and cheerful manner.

A hard frost had London in its grip. The earl ordered that the water pipes outside the town house were to be lagged with old sheets because he could see the burst pipes of less diligent owners glittering with long icicles.

Ailsa was leaving work one evening. She stopped outside a butcher's shop and looked up at the fat geese hanging from hooks.

A light pleasant voice behind her said, "Which one would you like?"

Ailsa turned round. In the light of the shop, she saw a fashionably dressed man with a dissipated face and his tall silk hat worn at a rakish angle.

"I am admiring the birds, sir," she said. "I will not be buying one."

"Going to be alone at Christmas?"

"Yes."

"Me, too. Look, it's dashed cold evening. Why don't you join me for a drink in that pub over there?"

Ailsa surveyed him from under the brim of her black felt

hat ornamented with a pheasant's feather. She had not had much to drink that day. Although Harry paid her a good salary, a large part of it went to an orphans' charity, some on food and rent and the rest on gin.

A pub was a public place. Nothing could happen to her there. Also, she was curious to find out why this man had waylaid her.

"Very well, sir," she said. "But just one. I have a weak head and I am not accustomed to strong liquor."

Guy Delancey felt relieved. Berrow had said to charm her, get her drunk and either get the office keys out of her reticule or make her so besotted with him that she would turn over the negative.

He took her arm and guided her across the road through the traffic, which had ground to a halt as usual. The newspapers were complaining that the whole of London was seized up with too much traffic.

He found a corner table in the pub. A waiter came bustling up. "What will you have, miss? Champagne?"

"No, I might try some gin. My mother used to like gin."

"Gin it is. Make it a large one, and I'll have a large whisky."

When the drinks arrived, Guy introduced himself. Ailsa thought of using a different name but then gave him her real one.

"Drink up," said Guy.

"My father always used to say, 'Bottoms up,' and drain his glass. I've never tried that."

"Let's try it now."

"Bottoms up," said Ailsa and knocked back her glass in one gulp. Guy followed suit.

He called the waiter and ordered another round. "That

poor waiter, running to and fro," said Ailsa. "Why does he not just bring the bottles?"

"Good idea!" Gosh, thought Guy, she'll be putty. A few more glasses and she'll do anything I want. He surveyed Ailsa with her flat chest, thin pale face and hooded eyes. Probably had nothing stronger than a glass of sweet sherry in all her life.

The waiter, as ordered, brought a bottle of whisky and a bottle of gin to the table.

"I'll be Mother," said Ailsa, just as if she were pouring tea instead of liquor. "Bottoms up!"

Guy soon began to feel his senses reeling. "I shay," he said, "where d'you work?"

"I work for an orphans' fund," said Ailsa. "This is fun. Bottoms up!"

"You mean you don't work for Captain Cashcart?"

"Never heard of him," said Ailsa. "Bottoms up!"

Guy lurched to his feet. He had made a dreadful mistake. He had followed her from the office in Buckingham Palace Road. But there were other offices there.

"Gotto go," he said thickly.

Ailsa watched as he staggered from the pub.

Lady Glensheil was late for a dinner party. She opened the trap on the roof of her carriage with her stick. "The traffic has cleared, John," she shouted to her coachman. "Go faster. Spring those horses."

"Very good, my lady."

Guy, lurching out of the pub onto the road, never saw the carriage hurtling towards him until it was too late.

At the sound of the scream and the crash, everyone ran out of the pub.

Ailsa gathered up her scarf, gloves and reticule and walked out. A carriage was lying on its side and an autocratic lady was being helped out. Guy was lying on the road, blood pouring from his head.

"Are the horses all right, John?" called Lady Glensheil.

"Yes, my lady."

"Thank goodness for that. I would not like to think good horseflesh had been ruined by some drunk."

The conspirators did not hear the bad news until they read the following day's *Evening News*. "Young man-about-town, Mr. Guy Delancey, was killed when he walked in front of Lady Glensheil's carriage. Witnesses say he had been drinking heavily in the Fox and Ferret with a lady. Police are urging his companion to come forward."

"And are you coming forward?" Harry asked Ailsa, who had told him the whole story.

"No, sir. Better just to leave it as it is."

"Quite right. Berrow and Banks probably hired someone to get you drunk. You say you were drinking water in a gin glass and he didn't even notice?"

"No, sir. He did not. I think he had a very weak head." Ailsa had no intention of betraying her capacity for gin to anyone.

Berrow and Cyril stared at each other in horror in The Club over their copies of the *Evening News*.

"You know what?" said Cyril.

"What?"

"That Cathcart fellow's going to kill both of us. He's engaged to Lady Rose again. I'm telling you, he's vicious."

Berrow folded his newspaper. "Tell you what, I'm going north to my place in Yorkshire for Christmas. Come along. We'll leave as soon as possible. If that maniac turns up anywhere near us, I'll get the keepers to shoot him!"

Rose, once again serving in the soup kitchen, found the cheerful religious man she had met before standing in front of her.

"The Lord be with you," he said, holding out his bowl.

"And with you, sir," said Rose.

"The Lord is good," he said, looking at her with shining eyes. "His angel come to me in prison."

"And you will sin no more?" asked Rose.

"Bet your life I won't, missus," he said cheerfully. "Can I have an extra helping?"

When she and Miss Friendly had finished, they returned to the town house where the maids were beginning to pack their trunks preparatory to the move to Stacey Court.

Before she went upstairs, Miss Friendly said, "Please tell Miss Levine I have her frock ready."

"I hope everyone is not taking advantage of you."

"No, not at all. I enjoy the work."

Daisy looked in awe at the dark blue taffeta gown Miss Friendly had designed and made for her. It was cut low on the bodice and trimmed with little pearls at the edge of the neckline.

"Did you do this without a pattern, Florence?" asked Daisy, who was the only one to call Miss Friendly by her first name.

"I studied such a gown when we were visiting Madame Laurent's salon and suddenly realized I could create something like it."

"You should speak to Lady Rose about opening your own salon."

"That would take a great deal of money and my lady has been generous enough."

Daisy thanked her and went off lost in thought. What if she, Becket and Miss Friendly got together to open a salon? She and Becket could handle the business side. Rose could be persuaded to wear Miss Friendly's creations as a form of advertisement. She and Becket could then marry.

Daisy wore the new gown that evening. Lady Polly kept flashing angry little glances at her. Harry had joined them for dinner.

Rose was feeling depressed. Harry was certainly playing his part of being the faithful fiancé, but there was something aloof and guarded about him when he spoke to her.

When Lady Polly led the ladies to the drawing-room after dinner, she glared again at Daisy's gown and said to her daughter, "You must not pass on your finest clothes to your companion. That gown is quite unsuitable."

"Miss Friendly designed and made it for her."

"You are sure?"

"Oh, yes."

"She could have her own salon and make a fortune," said Daisy.

"Miss Friendly has enough to do here," snapped the countess, looking enviously at the companion's gown. "I think she should start making clothes for me."

Two days later, the earl's household set out for the country. London was still in the grip of a great frost. As the line of carriages and fourgons moved out into the countryside, white trees and bushes lined the road. Everything seemed still and frozen. Smoke from cottage chimneys rose straight up into the darkening sky.

Rose huddled into her furs. She thought of Dolly now lying under the cold earth in her father's churchyard. Poor Dolly. If only she could find out who had murdered the girl, she felt that Dolly could rest in peace. The letters from Mrs. Tremaine had abruptly ceased, but Rose supposed that it was because she had stopped answering any of them.

Harry had promised to arrive on the following day. It had been very difficult to find a Christmas present for him. Rose had finally settled on buying him a copy of *The New Motoring Handbook*. Now she wished she had bought something more expensive, like a pair of gold cuff-links. The bottle of French scent she had bought for Daisy had cost a great deal more than the book.

She found she was missing her work at the soup kitchen. It had given some purpose to her days. She had persuaded her father to let her send six geese to the soup kitchen for Christmas dinners and felt she should have been there in person to serve them.

The work in the East End had made her look too closely at her own life for comfort. When they finally arrived at Stacey Court, all she had to do was go to her rooms and rest while an army of servants unloaded the fourgons, footmen carried up the trunks and maids unpacked the clothes.

She had suggested to her mother that such great divisions between rich and poor were worrying, but Lady Polly had merely pointed out that God put one in one's appointed station. If Rose wanted to continue with good works at Stacey Court, said the countess, then there were plenty of people in the village who would be glad of her services.

The next day she confided to Matthew Jarvis that sometimes she envied her parents' indifference to the poor. "Your father is not as indifferent as he seems. None of his tenants are allowed to starve or fall sick without treatment," said Matthew. "I have instructions to tell the factor not to collect any rent from the poorest."

Rose wrapped up her Christmas presents and put them on a table under the tree. The servants' hall had their own tree and presents would be given from the earl and countess at the servants' dance, traditionally held in the afternoon of Christmas day.

Harry arrived, polite, attentive and as closed as a shut door. Christmas came and went. Harry gave her a splendid diamond-and-sapphire necklace and she blushed when she handed him that book.

And then, after Boxing Day, one of the maids fell ill with typhoid and part of the drive fell into the cesspool below.

A doctor was summoned to treat the maid. A nurse was hired for her. The factor was instructed to deal with the cesspool and the earl thought it safer to remove everyone back to London.

As they arrived at the town house, it began to snow, small swirling flakes that seemed to rise upwards in the lamplight.

Fires were hurriedly lit. The house was freezing. Rose went to bed that night with two stone hot-water bottles in her bed, or "pigs," as they were called.

She was just drifting off to sleep, watching the flames dancing in the fireplace through half-closed lids, when suddenly she was wide awake.

At last she knew what it was that had been nagging at the back of her brain. She must tell Harry.

She was sure she now knew who had murdered Dolly.

In Yorkshire, Berrow and Cyril were feeling more like their horrible selves. They had shot every animal and bird on the estate that they could, had gone wenching in the brothels of York, and were beginning to regret having been so scared of Harry Cathcart.

It was only when the gamekeeper caught a poacher and dragged the man in to see Lord Berrow at gunpoint that Berrow began to have the germ of an idea. "I'll take him to the police," said the gamekeeper.

Berrow eyed the poacher thoughtfully. Most poachers were people who risked prison in order to feed their families during the hard winter, but this one was an unsavoury character with one wall eye, a long nose, and thin greasy hair. He dismissed the gamekeeper.

"Name," barked Berrow.

"John Finch, melord."

"Prison for you, me lad. What do you think of that?"

"Been there. Leastways get fed."

"What were you in prison for?"

"Beating the wife."

"Nonsense, man. Most men beat their wives, as is their right."

"Was living ower near place called Drifton. My Ruby cheeked me, so I took a plank to her. Local copper comes rushing in. Charges me with assault and battery. Thought they'd throw it out o' court but damned if they did. When I got out, Ruby was gone."

"You'll get life this time. Second offence."

Finch looked frightened but tried to cover it up with a pathetic attempt to swagger. "Well, go on. Get it over with."

Berrow studied him for a long moment.

"There could be another way."

Rose fretted. Harry had gone out of town on a case. London was buried under great drifts and there were reports that the Thames had frozen.

All she could do was wait impatiently for his return.

Ailsa Bridge lifted her skirt and extracted the flat flask she kept secured by her garter. She took a hearty swig and then began to type again. Harry had assured her that Berrow and Banks were in Yorkshire and that she would be safe from any other attempts.

Her life with her missionary parents in Burma had been full of danger and she had taken many great risks to supply the War Office in London with intelligence. She did not feel as confident as Harry and did not want to worry him. She had bought an old breastplate in an antique shop and was wearing it under her gown. She also had primed Harry's pistol and put it in her own desk.

She heard a step on the stair and stiffened. There was something furtive about that step. The nobility who usually frequented the office would come crashing in, full of bluster, demanding that some scandal or other be hushed up or some missing dog found.

Ailsa slid open the drawer and took out the pistol, laid it on top of the desk and covered it with her scarf.

The door opened and a man in a tweed coat, knickerbockers and a flat cap came in.

"Where's the captain?" he demanded.

"Out of town. Please leave."

He pulled out a gun and pointed it at her. "Go in there." He jerked his head at the inner office. "Open the safe."

Ailsa's hand crept towards the gun.

Finch saw the movement and shot her full in the chest. Ailsa crashed backwards in her chair and fell to the floor and lay still.

He searched in her desk until he found the keys. He went into the inner office and opened the safe. He was just reaching into it when a shot caught him on the shoulder. He grabbed his wounded shoulder and turned round. White-faced but stern, Ailsa was holding a pistol on him. He looked wildly for the gun, which he had put on Harry's desk, but keeping him covered, Ailsa picked it up and threw it onto the floor.

As he groaned and clutched his shoulder, she picked up the receiver and said in a crisp voice, "Police."

After she had made a statement to the police and they had left with Finch, Ailsa telephoned Harry. He listened in horror and said, "But you said he shot you!"

"I was wearing a breastplate," said Ailsa.

"You are sharper than I am. I'll come straight back. Meanwhile, you will find a negative and a photograph in the safe.

They are in an envelope. Do not look at them. I do not want the police to see them. Please call Phil Marshall and tell him to come and pick them up. The police did not find them, did they?"

"No, I told them he had no time to take anything."

"Go home, Miss Bridge. I shall go directly to Scotland Yard."

Harry was ushered in to see Kerridge. "This is a bad business," he said. "The chap who tried to kill your secretary is an unsavoury character called John Finch. He says he was hired by Lord Berrow, furnished with a gun, told to kill you if necessary and to get a negative out of your safe. We sent a man back and he retrieved the negative. It was nothing but a negative and photograph of a saucy lady in the altogether. Miss Bridge said a client of yours had paid you to get the negative and photo back. She said Berrow knew of the photograph and might use it to ruin her reputation."

Oh, excellent Miss Bridge, thought Harry.

"That is true. I never thought Berrow would go to such extremes. Furthermore I cannot, of course, give you the name of the lady. She has done nothing criminal. What are you doing about Berrow?"

"The police commissioner in York is going out to his estate to arrest him personally."

Oh, the magic of a title. If Lord Berrow had been Mr. Bloggs of nowhere, the police would have pounced without warning. But the police commissioner made the mistake of phoning Berrow first and saying he was coming to see him on a grave matter and bringing the chief constable with him.

Berrow rushed to find Cyril, who was potting balls in the billiard-room. Cyril had highly approved of the plot to hire Finch.

"We've got to get out of here," he said. "The game's up." He told Cyril about the impending visit of the police commissioner and the chief constable.

"What'll we do?"

"Get out the bloody country, that's what!"

NINE

++

Life is the art of drawing sufficient conclusions from insufficient premises.

— SAMUEL BUTLER

Berrow and Cyril fled as far as Glasgow. Scottish law was different from English law, so surely, they felt, they would feel safe for a while.

They booked into the Central Hotel beside the railway station, sharing a suite and calling themselves the brothers Richmond.

"I say," said Cyril moodily, looking at their great pile of luggage, "we are drawing attention to ourselves with all this stuff. We had to employ a squad of porters to get the few yards round from the station. And I'm sick of this disguise. It's hot." Like Berrow, Cyril was sporting a false beard. They had managed to work their way north by means of several branch railway lines before they arrived tired and weary in Glasgow.

"I've got an idea," said Berrow. "You know that big motor car Cathcart has?"

"What about it?"

"We could get something like that. It would take us and all

the luggage. We could then make our way by country roads to Stranraer, get over to Ireland. Great place to hide out, Ireland."

Both had taken with them a considerable amount of money and valuables. The timely warning call from the police had also enabled them to transfer their accounts to a Swiss bank.

"Good idea," said Cyril.

That evening, they inquired at the reception desk for the whereabouts of a motor car salesroom and got directions to a large one in Giffnock.

The following morning, they set out. Pride of the salesroom display was a Rolls-Royce, and Berrow decided that it would be ideal. He paid cash, to the delight of the salesman, who then discovered that neither knew how to drive.

Cyril was taken out on the road for a lesson. After two hours, he decided he knew how to start up and go forward. So long as he was not expected to reverse, he felt he could manage pretty well. They returned to the centre of the city and bought leather motoring coats, leather hats and goggles, and Berrow embellished his ensemble with a long white silk scarf.

Not wanting to cope with the Glasgow traffic, they took a cab back to their hotel. They waited until the following morning and had to hire two of Glasgow's new motorized taxi-cabs to take them and their luggage out to the salesroom.

With Cyril at the wheel, scowling in concentration, they set out on the road. Berrow studied ordnance survey maps. The idea was to go by country roads to Stranraer and take the ferry to Ireland. They planned to hide out in Ireland for a time and then sail to France and make their way to Switzerland.

The weather was fine, with feathery clouds decorating a pale blue sky. The fresh scents of the countryside blew into the open car. Cyril relaxed as he grew more confident.

The trouble began when they motored through a village and a pretty girl stared at the car in open-mouthed admiration.

When they were clear of the village and Berrow saw a long straight stretch of road ahead, he called, "Stop!" Berrow had become jealous of Cyril at the wheel.

Cyril pulled to a halt. "What's up?"

"Let me take the wheel for a bit."

"You can't drive."

"Show me. Just how to move it along."

"Oh, all right." Cyril got out and they changed places.

After several attempts and crashing gears, Berrow managed to get the car to move forward. He pressed his foot down on the accelerator. Although the speed limit was thirty miles an hour, the Rolls was capable of doing a hundred.

Hedges hurtled past in a blur as Cyril screamed, "Ease off the accelerator!"

"What?" shouted Berrow. "This is fun."

As he hurtled down a bend in the road and straight at a hump-backed bridge, his scarf blew across his face. Panicking, Cyril grabbed the wheel. With a great crash, the car hit the parapet sideways on. The ancient stonework crumpled. Cyril was catapulted onto the river bank. He hit a stone with the full impact of his head and lay still.

Berrow stared down at him in horror. "Are you all right?" he called, but he was sure Cyril was dead.

He felt the car lurch. He got out carefully and went and looked at the damage. The wheels were hanging over the edge where the parapet had once been.

He struggled down the river bank to Cyril. He felt for a pulse but found none.

Berrow climbed back to the car. He would need to walk back to that village for help. His hands were shaking. He stood at the back of the car, lit a cigarette with a vesta and tossed the lighted match on the ground, unaware of the lake of petrol that had formed.

There was a terrific explosion as Berrow and the car went up in a fireball of flame.

Harry was to escort Rose to a luncheon party and she prayed he would not cancel.

They were accompanied by Daisy, Turner, the lady's maid, and two footmen. Rose began to wonder if she would ever have a chance to speak to Harry in private.

She was not seated next to him at table and so talked a little to the gentleman on her right—the weather—and the gentleman on her left—the state of the nation—picked at her food and thought the wretched meal with its eight courses would never end. How wonderful it would be, she thought, if I were to pick up the table-cloth and bundle all this food and take it down to the East End.

At last the hostess signalled to the ladies to join her in the drawing-room and leave the gentlemen to their port.

"Why are you looking so nervous?" whispered Daisy.

"Nothing." Rose wanted to tell Harry about her discovery first. A little twinge of guilt warned her that she should have confided in Daisy first, but Rose wanted to impress Harry, to show him she could detect as well.

At last the gentlemen came in. Bridge tables were being set

up and Daisy's green eyes gleamed like a cat's. She was a killing bridge player.

Harry joined Rose. She whispered urgently, "I must talk to you in private."

"There's a conservatory at the back of the house. Let's walk there."

In the steamy warmth of the conservatory, they sat down on a bench in front of a marble statue of Niobe.

Harry was the first to speak. Rose listened in amazement when he told her how Berrow and Banks had hired Finch and how his secretary had nearly been killed. "The police commissioner in York is going to arrest them. Don't you see? You are safe now. They must have been the ones behind the murder of Dolly."

Rose's splendid deduction was losing its glow, but she said, "I have discovered something as well. I am sure it was Jeremy Tremaine who hired Reg Bolton."

"Why?"

"There is this Cockney who comes to the soup kitchen. He found God in prison. Don't you see? Jeremy is a divinity student. He could have been visiting prisoners and found a useful one."

"I really do think we'll find out it was Berrow and Banks."

Rose looked so disappointed that he said hurriedly, "To put your mind at rest, I can leave now and go to Wormwood Scrubs and check the book for visiting clerics."

"Take me with you. Please!"

"Very well. Tell Daisy to take Turner home in a cab."

Normally Daisy would have been curious, but she was so addicted to cards that she only nodded.

———

At the prison, the governor protested that he was too busy a man to keep dealing with Captain Cathcart's requests.

Rose gave him a blinding smile and the governor thawed. He not only produced the required books but suggested that he take Rose on a tour of the prison.

Wormwood Scrubs proved to be even larger than Rose had imagined. It generally contained a thousand male and two hundred female convicts. They walked round the laundries where the women worked and then to the bakeries where the prisoners in their ugly uniforms were baking bread. There was also shoemaking and tailoring going on.

What Rose found unnerving was that all the labour was done in complete silence. It was like being in a Trappist monastery.

She was also taken to a room where the triangles were. Prisoners were strapped to these triangles and either birched or lashed with the cat-o'-nine-tails. The cat-o'-nine-tails was kept in a drawer. The governor lifted it out for Rose to examine. "Doesn't look much, but it can inflict some damage."

Rose repressed a shudder and suggested they return to Harry.

He was just closing the books when they entered the governor's barrack-like office.

As he and Rose got into the Rolls, he said, "Jeremy Tremaine visited the prison on six occasions in the months before his sister's death. One of the prisoners he visited was Reg Bolton."

"I wonder what Jeremy will say when we ask him?"

"We? I thought of going myself with Becket tomorrow."

"You must take me with you! It was my idea."

"I suppose your parents will agree if we take Becket and Daisy."

Lady Polly was in a fury when they got back, demanding to know where they had gone, Rose without either her maid or companion. Rose took Harry's arm and smiled up at him. "Only for a little drive," she said. "We wanted to be alone."

Harry's heart gave a lurch and then he realized that, of course, she was acting.

Nonetheless, it took a great deal of persuading to get permission to go "for a little drive" with Harry the following day with just Becket and Daisy as chaperones.

But Lady Polly finally melted. She saw the way Rose smiled up at the captain and was sure her wayward daughter was in love at last.

They all set out the following morning in high spirits that even the damp mist clouding the day could not dim.

Daisy had won too much at cards to be angry with Rose for not having told her about Jeremy.

When they turned down Oxford High, the mist was hiding the spires and pinnacles of the colleges, and even the top of Cairfax Tower was lost to view.

Daisy and Becket were told to stay in the car while Rose and Harry made their way up the shallow stone steps to Jeremy's rooms.

"We're in luck," said Harry. "He's not sporting his oak."

"What does that mean?"

"These are double doors. If the outer door is closed, that's called sporting the oak and it means you're either out or do not want visitors."

Harry knocked and a faint voice called, "Enter."

Harry held open the door for Rose and followed her in. Jeremy was dressed in gown and mortar board.

"What do you want?" he demanded harshly. "I was just going out."

"You visited a certain Reg Bolton in Wormwood Scrubs on several occasions just before his release. He is the man who tried twice to kill Lady Rose."

"I visited him along with other prisoners. I was doing my duty, bringing Christian hope to the suffering."

"Nobody seems to think of bringing Christian hope to the victims," said Rose.

"Don't you think it odd," pursued Harry, "that after your sister is murdered, a hired assassin called Reg Bolton tries to kill Lady Rose, a man you visited?"

Jeremy's face was wax-pale and his eyes burned with fury. "Get out of here," he shouted. "How *dare* you? You are accusing me of killing my own sister."

"You haven't heard the end of this," said Harry. "I am sure the police will want to interview you. Come, Rose."

"Well, I didn't expect to get a confession out of him," said Rose as they walked together across the quadrangle.

"No, the purpose was to rattle him and see if he betrays himself in any way."

Daisy and Becket sat in the front seat in sulky silence. Becket had sprung the idea on Daisy that maybe they could one day save enough to buy a little pub in the country. Daisy could work behind the bar. Daisy had said furiously that she was not going to sink to be a barmaid. Becket had called her a snob and said she had acquired ideas above her station.

175

Becket was driving, so Rose and Harry climbed into the back.

They went to the Randolph Hotel for luncheon. Daisy and Becket sat at a separate table, staring angrily at each other in dead silence.

"I think," said Harry, "that I should go to Scotland Yard on our return and tell Kerridge about these visits."

"Good idea. I shall come with you."

"I'm afraid not."

"Why?"

"It's a man's world. There are people at Scotland Yard who view my visits with disfavour. They feel Kerridge should not be wasting time with amateurs. The presence of even a beautiful lady like yourself diminishes me."

"That's not fair!"

"As I have just pointed out to you, it's man's world."

Now Rose was, like her companion, too furious to speak. Harry tried several times to talk about various things, but she sat glaring at him and refused to utter a word.

It was a carload of silent and sulky people who returned to London.

Harry went straight to Scotland Yard. Kerridge was out on a case, so he waited patiently while the mist thickened on the river Thames outside the window.

At last Kerridge returned and listened in surprise to Harry's story about Jeremy's prison visits.

"I'll pull him in for questioning."

"It won't do any good at the moment. All he has to do is look outraged. No one else is going to believe he had a hand in his sister's murder. I'd like to examine that house they rented for the Season."

"What do you expect to find? It'll have been scrubbed from top to bottom."

"There might just be something."

"All right. I'll come along with you."

"Are you sure the servants that were there at the time didn't hear or see anything?"

"With the exception of a temporary footman hired from an agency, the servants were all the country ones. I gather Apton Magna is a pretty poor place. They weren't going to say anything that might mean they'd lose their jobs."

The thin house in Clarges Street that had been rented by the Tremaines was standing empty. They got the key from the factor and let themselves in, then searched high and low, Harry crawling along the floor-boards, to see if one blood-stain might have been overlooked.

"She might have been killed here," said Harry. "She certainly wasn't killed in that boat or there would have been a lot more blood."

"The pathologist said that costume had been put on her after her death and the blood from the wound on her chest had seeped through the material."

"You didn't tell me that."

"You're not in the force and I have plenty of other cases taking up my time, which reminds me, if you're finished here I'd like to get back to the Yard."

"I hate being passed over just because I'm a woman," raged Rose, walking up and down her sitting-room. "I'd like to show him I can detect better than he can. I'd like to go down to Apton Magna and get the parents' reaction to the fact that their precious son was consorting with a criminal. But how are we to get out of the house without Turner and two footmen following us?"

"I've an idea," said Daisy. "'Member that ladder we used to get over the garden wall? It's at the side of the garden. If we left, say, about five in the morning, the staff would still be asleep. We could sneak out and get the early-morning train at Paddington."

"We'll do it!" said Rose.

Harry set out to find the temporary footman who had worked for the Tremaines. His name was Will Hubbard and his address was number five Sweetwater Lane in the City.

After the Great Fire, plans had been drawn up to build a modern City out of the ashes, with airy streets and wide boulevards. But there turned out to be so many claims from property owners who would demand heavy compensation if, say, a street ran through where their buildings used to be, that the new City, the commercial hub of London, rose again following the old medieval pattern of narrow winding lanes.

Sweetwater Lane was just north of Ludgate Circus and consisted of two lines of black tenements. Number five had a great quantity of bell-pulls. Harry pulled several of them. The front door was opened by a lever on each landing. When the door opened, several voices asked him what he wanted.

"Will Hubbard," he shouted. There was a sudden silence and then the sound of slamming doors.

He made his way up, knocking on door after door, but nobody answered until, at the very top, an elderly lady opened the door a little. "I am Captain Cathcart," said Harry. "I am helping Scotland Yard with an investigation."

The door began to close. He put his foot in it, fished out a guinea and held it up. The door opened wide. She snatched the guinea in a claw-like hand.

"Come in. What do you want?"

The room was sparsely furnished with a table and two chairs and an iron bedstead in the corner. A linnet in a wicker cage sang at the window.

"Do you know where I can find William Hubbard?"

"In the cemetery."

"What happened?"

" 'Twere a good few months ago. I heard shouting and then a scream. That was during the night. But there's often screaming and shouting here. In the morning, I went out to buy milk. He lived in the room below this one. The door was standing open and he was lying there, all blood. He'd been stabbed.

"I was ever so shook. I went out and saw a policeman and told him. More police came and then detectives. But nobody said anything. Well, most of them are villains, so they wouldn't. Then his pore sister came. Such a taking she was in. I took her up to my room and made her tea."

"Do you know where she lives?"

"She wrote it down on a slip of paper and told me if I remembered anything at all to contact her."

"Do you still have it?"

She went over to the mantelpiece and extracted a piece of paper from behind a plaster statue of the Virgin Mary.

"May I take this?"

"Yes, I've no use for it. I couldn't tell her any more than I've told you."

Outside, Harry looked at the paper. A Miss Emily Hubbard was lady's maid to a Mrs. Losse and there was an address in Launceston Place in Kensington.

He drove to Launceston Place and rang the bell. When a butler answered, Harry handed him his card and said he wished to speak to Miss Hubbard.

"Wait there," said the butler, letting him into a hall which was little more than a narrow passage.

Harry waited. Then the butler came back downstairs, followed by a vision. This surely could not be the lady's maid.

"Captain Cathcart," she cooed in a husky voice with a slight accent. "I've always wanted to meet you. I am Mrs. Losse. Please come into the parlour and tell me why you want to speak to Emily."

Mrs. Losse had masses of glossy auburn hair piled up on her small head. Her excellent bosom and tiny waist were displayed to advantage in a green silk gown which matched her very large and sparkling green eyes.

She listened while Harry told her of the murder of William Hubbard. "I feel it is connected to another case I am investigating."

"How thrilling. I read about you in the newspapers. So brave! All those people you rescued in that dreadful train crash." They were sitting together on a sofa. She put her hand on his arm and leaned towards him. She was wearing a heady perfume. Harry thought briefly of his chilly fiancée with a flash of dislike.

"May I speak to Miss Hubbard?" asked Harry. Something seemed to have happened to his voice and it came out as a croak. She gave him a languorous smile and rang a little silver bell on the table in front of her.

After a moment, a mousy little woman entered the room. She was in complete contrast to the amazing beauty of her mistress. Harry wondered whether she had been employed for that very reason.

"You may be seated, Emily," said Mrs. Losse. "This is Captain Cathcart. He has decided to investigate further the murder of your poor brother."

Emily sat down on the very edge of a chair and clasped her hands. "Oh, sir," she said, "I was afraid no one was ever going to find out anything."

"Tell me about your brother?" asked Harry gently.

"He was good and worked hard. He liked working for the agency because he said there were so many banquets and functions that there was always demand for extra footmen and he didn't need to be tied to one master like some."

I wonder whether he was blackmailing the Tremaines, thought Harry. Aloud, he asked, "Did your brother say anything about coming into money?"

She gave a sad little laugh. "He was always dreaming. I met him just before he was killed on my day off. We walked down to London Bridge. He said we would go and buy a little cottage in the country and raise hens and pigs."

"And was this new?"

She sighed. "Oh, no, it was a dream he'd always had."

"Did he talk of any rich or influential friends?"

"No, sir. He only talked about other servants he had met on his various jobs."

Harry promised that if he found out anything, he would let her know immediately. Emily was dismissed. Harry rose to leave.

"You must come back and see me," said Mrs. Losse as she escorted him to the door. She stood very close to him in the narrow passage, that bewitching face of hers turned up to his own.

"Yes, I will," said Harry.

"Promise!" Those eyes glinted flirtatiously. Harry laughed. "Of course."

He went straight to Scotland Yard to find that Kerridge had gone home ages ago and so he said he would return in the morning. When he returned to his home, he told Becket of the latest developments.

"Do you not think you should tell Lady Rose about this?" suggested Becket.

"No, I don't think so. She will demand again to accompany me to Scotland Yard. I am in enough difficulties there with some of them who regard me as an interfering amateur. Lady Rose is very forceful. With her along, it would look as if I was under some sort of petticoat government and life would be made even more difficult for me. Kerridge is always helpful, but he doesn't tell me everything just because I am not on the force. I know that Inspector Judd disapproves of me and I have overheard detectives calling me 'that dilettante.' I shall call on her after I have talked to Kerridge."

"It is late," said Becket. "You were supposed to take dinner with the Hadfields this evening."

"Now I really am in trouble," groaned Harry.

"I really think it shameful," said Lady Polly over dinner that evening. "Captain Cathcart now no longer calls to give his excuses. I am furious with him and so I shall tell him."

"I hope he is all right," said Daisy. "I am sure it was something very important."

Mrs. Barrington-Bruce was one of the guests. She gave a great laugh. "To be sure, for a man it was important."

"Do you know something?" asked Rose.

"Only that one of my footmen was walking my little doggies round Launceston Place. He told me just before I left to come here that he had seen Captain Cathcart visiting the home of a certain Mrs. Josse."

"Who is Mrs. Josse?" asked Rose.

"A certain very beautiful member of the demi-monde."

"Then it must be part of some case the captain was working on," said Rose.

Mrs. Barrington-Bruce looked at her with pity in her eyes. "Oh, my poor child. My poor *innocent* child."

Rose was so angry that she barely slept that night, but she was still determined to go to Apton Magna. She rehearsed scene after scene in her mind where she would present Kerridge with evidence that Jeremy was a murderer, and leave the superintendent to let Harry know she had solved the case.

At five in the morning, she and Daisy crept downstairs and into the back garden. They propped the ladder against the wall and climbed up. They sat on the top and pulled up the ladder and slid it down the other side.

Once they were in the lane, they hurried away. Beyond the square, they were lucky in finding a sleepy cabbie, and asked him to take them to Paddington Station, where Rose bought two first-class tickets.

Once the train moved out, Daisy fell asleep, her head bobbing against the lace antimacassar. Rose sat bolt upright, staring unseeingly at a bad oil painting of the coastal town of Deal on the carriage wall opposite.

The carriage was stuffy, so she jerked down the window by the leather strap. The train plunged into a tunnel and smoke billowed into the carriage. She spluttered and choked and jerked the window shut again.

When a waiter called out that breakfast was served, Rose shook Daisy awake and they made their way to the dining-car.

They ate in silence. Daisy was beginning to wonder if Becket would make a suitable husband after all and Rose was eaten up with fury at Harry.

At Oxford, they changed onto the train for Moreton-in-Marsh. It coughed and wheezed and jerked its slow way into little country stations and then sat at each for what seemed like ages before jerking forward again.

They found a cab in the forecourt of Moreton-in-Marsh Station. Rose instructed him to take them to the rectory at Apton Magna and to wait for them.

"It's Sunday," said Daisy. "They'll all probably be in church."

As they got down from the carriage, they could see the congregation filing into church.

Inside, the pews were like the ones in railway carriages. "Let's go up to the gallery," whispered Rose. "We'll get a better look from there."

They sat in the front of the gallery and looked down. A smell of unwashed poverty rose up from the well of the church and Rose held a scented handkerchief to her nose.

"I wonder," she murmured to Daisy, "why the rector ended up in a poor living like this. Perhaps there is something in his past which put him out of favour."

They got to their feet for the opening hymn. As they sang, Rose saw the rector in his robes walking down the aisle. He climbed up the steps to the pulpit, grasped the wings of the golden eagle which decorated the pulpit and stared down at the congregation.

"Look!" hissed Rose when the hymn finished. Jeremy Tremaine was walking down to a lectern under the pulpit.

Jeremy began reading from the Revelation of Saint John the Divine.

"And he that sat was to look upon like a jasper and a sardine stone: and there was a rainbow round about the throne, in sight like unto an emerald."

"What's a sardine stone?" asked Daisy.

"Shhh!"

Jeremy's voice droned soporifically on. "And I looked, and behold a pale horse: and his name that sat upon him was Death."

He cast his eyes up piously and then they suddenly sharpened and focused directly on Rose and Daisy. He slammed the Bible shut and strode off down the aisle. His father looked down in surprise at his son's retreating figure and then looked at the gallery. When he saw them, for a brief moment his face was a mask of fury.

Then the next hymn began.

The lady's maid, Turner, waited to be summoned by Rose. When no summons came, she went to Rose's bedchamber. Finding it empty, she checked the sitting-room and then Daisy's room.

Turner became very worried. Only the other day, Lady Polly had threatened her with dismissal if she tried to cover up what Rose was doing.

She went down to the breakfast room. "My lady," she said,

"Lady Rose is not in her rooms. Neither is Miss Levine."

The earl and countess stared at her in alarm.

Brum gave a discreet cough. "The coachman was saying this morning that the ladder that was left in the garden was now in the lane by the mews. Also there are footprints of ladies' boots in the mud in the mews."

"Damn the girl!" roared the earl. "Get Cathcart!"

As they both walked down from the gallery, Rose said, "This, I feel, is a dangerous mistake. I think we should leave."

"Me, too," said Daisy, heaving a sigh of relief.

They had to wait in line. The parishioners were shaking hands with the rector at the church door.

When it came their turn, Rose put out her hand and said, "We were in the neighbourhood and thought we would visit your charming church."

She held out her hand, determined to give his a brief shake and move out to the waiting carriage as quickly as possible. But he held her hand in a firm grip. "You must stay and take some refreshment. Ah, here is my wife. Mrs. Tremaine, do take the ladies indoors."

"I am afraid we really must go," said Rose, trying to extricate her hand. "Our carriage is waiting."

He turned round. "I do not see any carriage."

Rose stared across in dismay. "I told him to wait. No matter. It is a fine day for a walk. Come, Daisy."

"Now, you cannot walk," said Mrs. Tremaine. "Do but step inside the rectory and our carriage will take you."

She looked her normal friendly self. I'm imagining things, thought Rose.

"Very well. Just for a few moments. Most kind of you."

Harry was telling Kerridge about the murder of Will Hubbard. "That's too much of a coincidence," said Kerridge. "We'll go down there and sweat it out of those servants after we arrest the Tremaines. If they see the master arrested, then I think they might talk."

Judd entered and said lugubriously. "Lord Hadfield has just called. He wishes Captain Cathcart to attend him immediately."

"I am busy at the moment. Is all well with Lady Rose?"

"He says his daughter has disappeared. The staff believe she left during the night by climbing over the garden wall."

"Now what?" Harry looked at Kerridge in dismay. "Where would she go?"

"I hope it's anywhere but Apton Magna."

"Oh dear. I have an awful feeling that's just where she would go. She wanted to come here this morning and I wouldn't let her. Lady Rose, being as stubborn as a mule, has probably decided to investigate the Tremaines for herself." He turned to Judd. "Tell Lord Hadfield I am sure I know where his daughter has gone. I am going to collect her. Kerridge, we'll take my car. It's faster."

"I'll phone the Oxford police to get out there."

"No," said Harry. "If the Tremaines are guilty, something might happen to them if the police go crashing in first. We'll call on them in Oxford and get them to follow us."

"How kind of you to visit us again," twittered Mrs. Tremaine over the teacups. "Such an honour."

The rector and his son said nothing.

"Most kind of you," said Rose, "but we really must leave."

"Our carriage will be here shortly. Have another cake."

Daisy's green eyes were wide and frightened. Why did I come here? thought Rose desperately. No one knows we are here. But what can they do? I am not now going to ask Jeremy about his prison visits.

The rector spoke at last. "Who were you visiting in the neighbourhood?"

"We weren't really visiting anyone," said Rose. "The countryside here is so pretty, and after London, we felt in the need of fresh air."

"I am surprised," said Mrs. Tremaine, "that a great lady such as yourself should travel into the country in a hired cab with only your companion."

"I do like a little freedom sometimes. Now we really must go. If the carriage is not ready, we will walk." She got to her feet. "Come, Daisy."

"Just another moment or two," said Mrs. Tremaine. "I am still mourning my poor daughter. Why, only the other day, I found a number of Dolly's things in one of the attics. It turns out the poor girl kept a diary."

Rose decided this was too good a chance to miss. "Perhaps I may see her diary?"

"By all means. Follow me."

"You wait there, Daisy," said Rose.

"I'm coming with you."

Mrs. Tremaine led the way to the top of the house. She opened a low door and stood inside. "Go ahead. You will find her things in here."

Rose and Daisy walked into the room. As the door slammed behind them and the key turned in the lock, Rose realized they had been tricked.

They hammered on the door and screamed and shouted.

Surely one of the servants would hear them. But they had not seen any servants. Mrs. Tremaine had made and served tea herself.

"Jeremy!" said Rose. "He must have run out of the church and dismissed the servants for the day. Then he must have told his mother what he planned. I don't think she was in church when we arrived. She must have turned up towards the end of the service."

"The window's barred," said Daisy. "We've got to get out of here."

They sat in silence and then Rose whispered, "Listen. I can hear voices. It's coming from the fireplace."

They both crouched down beside the tiny fireplace. They could hear the voices of the Tremaine family. Jeremy was saying, "We must make sure they came on their own. I am sure her family doesn't know she is here."

Then Mrs. Tremaine: "I will take the pony and trap and go to the public phone-box in Moreton and phone the earl's household. I will say I am still distressed over Dolly's death and must speak to Lady Rose."

"You will just be told she is not at home." The rector's voice.

"I am a very good actress," said his wife. "Leave it to me."

The voices faded.

Rose and Daisy looked at each other in alarm. "Please God, Brum just says I am not at home without elaborating. They daren't do anything to us if they think anyone knows we are here."

Daisy's voice choked on a sob. "I was so nasty to Becket. If I ever see him again, I'll give him a great big kiss."

———

Mrs. Tremaine asked the telephone operator to connect her to the earl's residence. Brum answered. "May I speak to Lady Rose?" asked Mrs. Tremaine in a quavering voice.

"I am afraid Lady Rose is not at home."

"Oh dear," wailed Mrs. Tremaine. "Lady Rose has been helping me get over my terrible grief. I-I d-don't know what to do."

The inveterate gossip in Brum rose to the surface. He lowered his voice. "Between you and me, madam, Lady Rose sneaked out this morning and nobody knows where she is. Always wilful, she is."

"Oh, thank you. I will call again."

"I hear a carriage coming back," said Rose. They both crouched down by the fireplace again.

The chimney must lead straight down to the parlour, thought Rose, because she could clearly hear Mrs. Tremaine say, "The butler said she sneaked out this morning and nobody knows where she is."

"Good," came Jeremy's voice. "We'd better wait until dark."

Rose looked wildly round the attic room. "We've got to get out of here. They must be really mad. If anything happened to us, the captain would think immediately of Apton Magna and check all the cabbies at the station."

Daisy went over and put her eye to the keyhole. "They've left the key on the other side. Maybe I can poke it out. We need a piece of paper or cardboard to slide under the door."

"There's that old trunk over there. I'll lift the lid and see if we can find anything useful." She threw back the lid. "Schoolbooks. Just the thing." She tore the cardboard cover off one of the books and gave it to Daisy.

Daisy slipped the cardboard under the door and then took a hat-pin out of her hat and poked at the lock. "It's no good," she said at last, sitting back on her heels. "I need a straight piece of metal. I know, me stays."

Daisy took off her coat and frock and Rose helped her out of her corset. Then Rose took a little pair of scissors out of her reticule and they unpicked stitches and slid out one of the steels. Daisy put her corset and frock and coat back on again and set to work on the lock. An hour passed while Rose fretted, until Daisy said, "Got it!"

She drew the cardboard from under the door with the key on it.

"Quietly now," said Rose. "Let's take our boots off."

They slipped off their boots. Daisy gently unlocked the door and then locked it again behind them.

Holding their boots, they crept down the stairs. The house was silent. "Back door," murmured Daisy.

They walked softly down to the basement, opened the back door and let themselves out into the garden. They put their boots on and went out through the garden gate and began to run across the fields.

Rose finally stopped running. "We'd better circle round to the main road or we'll be lost."

"There's a farmhouse over there," said Daisy. "Let's go there and get someone to get the police."

"I don't trust anyone," said Rose. "The farmer is probably a tenant of the Tremaines and would tell them first. If we bear left, we should meet the road to Moreton."

They trudged on, always looking fearfully to the left and right.

At last they reached the road. "Now I feel free," said Rose as they both strode out in the direction of Moreton.

They rounded a bend in the road and Rose let out a scream of dismay. Jeremy and his father were just emerging from a copse.

They ran towards them. "Get the maid," shouted the rector. "I'll get the other."

Daisy shrieked in fright as Jeremy reached for her, and kicked him as hard in the crotch as she could. He doubled up and fell on the road. Rose seized a hat-pin out of her hat and drove it into the rector's arm. Undeterred, he threw his arms round her and began to drag her towards the trees. Daisy jumped on his back and clawed at his eyes.

The Rolls, speeding round the corner, nearly ran into them. Harry slammed on the brakes and leaped from the car. The rector released Rose and stood with his head hanging while Daisy slid off his back. She saw Becket climbing out of the back of the car and threw herself into his arms and kissed him full on the mouth.

A carload of police which had been following Harry's car came to a stop. Father and son were cautioned and handcuffed.

Overcome with relief, Rose ran to Harry. "You silly girl," he said furiously. "You could have been killed."

Rose, who had been about to throw herself into his arms, backed off. Her face flamed. "You would never have found out it was them if it hadn't been for me," she raged. Then she burst into tears.

"Oh, I'm sorry," said Harry. "I was so worried about you."

He tried to take her in his arms, but she turned away.

Daisy moved forwards and put an arm around Rose. "Quietly, now, my dear," she said. "It's all over now."

EPILOGUE

⚜

Once more, methought, I saw them stand

('Twas but a dream I know),

That elegant and noble band

Of fifty years ago.

The men, frock-coated, tall and proud,

The women in a silken cloud,

While in the midst of them appeared

(A vision I still retain)

The Monarch sipping pink champagne,

And smiling through his beard.

—JAMES LAVER

The Tremaine family were interviewed at Scotland Yard separately. Harry was given permission to sit in on the interviews.

All were claiming that they had been overset by Dolly's death and outraged by Lady Rose's visit, thinking she was prodding and prying and opening the fresh wounds of their grief.

During a break in the interviewing, Harry drew Kerridge aside. "I think you should point out to Jeremy that unless he owns up to murder, his mother and father will hang as well as himself."

"I think he's the toughest one of the three," said Kerridge. "Oh, by the way. Berrow and Banks have been found."

"Where? How?"

"About forty miles south of Glasgow. They were driving and their motor hit a bridge. Banks was thrown clear but hit a stone and was killed outright. The motor with Berrow went up in flames, so the state is spared two expensive trials. Banks had been stripped naked, probably by the locals. The police did a house-to-house search in the nearby village but found nothing. They probably buried the stuff somewhere and will dig it up later when they think the heat's died down. Berrow must have taken the wheel after the village because the locals did say that it was Banks at the wheel when they drove through."

"Good riddance," said Harry. "Let's try Jeremy again."

As they entered the interview room, Harry was struck afresh by the difference in looks between Jeremy and his beautiful sister.

Jeremy looked at them with flat eyes, sitting hunched at a table. He had refused a lawyer, saying he was innocent.

"I do not think you understand the gravity of the situation, Mr. Tremaine," began Kerridge. He sat down opposite Jeremy; Judd joined him and Harry sat in the corner of the room beside a policeman with a shorthand pad.

"I have done nothing wrong," said Jeremy. "God is my witness."

"Do you realize that because of your silence, you will all hang? Do you want to know that you sent your parents to a shameful death?"

"There is no proof."

"Your servants are talking now. On the night Dolly was killed, they heard her screaming, 'No! Don't!' We have the proof that you visited Reg Bolton in prison. He had money in his wallet. I am sure we can trace it to your bank. You killed the footman, Will Hubbard, or had Bolton do it for you. The police are interviewing everyone in Sweetwater Lane armed with photographs of you and of Bolton. But until there is actual proof that you yourself killed your sister, there will be enough circumstantial evidence to hang the lot of you."

Jeremy buried his head in his hands.

Harry suddenly spoke from his corner. "Had she been your own sister, you would not have killed her. But she was not your real sister, was she? Out with it, man. Confession is good for the soul, and you will be double-damned if you let your parents hang."

Jeremy began to sob. They waited patiently. At last he dried his eyes on his sleeve. "All right," he said in a weary voice. "All right. I'll tell you.

"It was Father's fault to start with. He had a good parish in Oxfordshire. But he got one of our servant girls pregnant. He had the living from Lord Dyrecombe. The girl went to Lady Dyrecombe. My father said it was her word against his, but the girl was the daughter of one of the Dyrecombes' respected tenants and they believed her. My father was told to look for another living. The bishop was angry with him and Apton Magna was all that was on offer. After the baby was born, the servant girl drowned herself and Lady Dyrecombe called on my father and said the least we could do was to bring the baby up as our own.

"My father had little to do with her until he noticed that she had become a great beauty. We all saw a way to restore our prestige and fortunes through Dolly. My father had received an inheritance and we decided to give Dolly a Season in London. She said she was in love with the blacksmith's son, but we told her she owed us everything."

He spoke in a dull, flat monotone. For a moment the only sound was the policeman's pencil catching up on his shorthand notes.

Jeremy sighed and began to speak again.

"Then Lord Berrow asked leave to pay his addresses. We told her he would be calling in the morning and she was to accept. We had such hopes. Berrow had spoken to me. He said once he was married to Dolly and I had finished my studies at Oxford, he could get me a good living, maybe even in Mayfair. He also said he would speak to the archbishop and get my father somewhere better than Apton Magna. We were so full of hope. We were so happy.

"Then Dolly began to scream that she would not do it, that she was going to run away. She went to her room.

"My parents sent me to see her. She defied me. She dared to laugh in my face. Me! That cuckoo in our family nest, that *bastard*, dared to laugh at me. I was blind with rage. I went to my room and got a dagger, a Turkish one, that someone had given me.

"I went back to her room and held it on her. 'You will do as you're told,' I said, 'or I will kill you.'

"She laughed again. 'You! You're not a man like my Roger,' she said. 'You wouldn't dare.' "

"That's when I stabbed her. There was blood everywhere. My parents came rushing in.

"We knew we had to get her away from the house. At the ball we'd seen her slipping a note to Lady Rose, and we stole it. We knew she planned to meet Lady Rose at the Serpentine. We thought, let Lady Rose find the body. With luck they'll think she did it.

"We'd had that Lady of Shalott costume made for her,

because her engagement was to be announced at the fancy-dress party the following week. We cleaned her and dressed her in it. I got the carriage round from the mews, and we put her in it and took her down to the Serpentine and laid her out in that rowing-boat. My father said prayers over her. Somehow it eased the horror to see her lying there so calm and beautiful.

"In the morning, we gathered all the servants together. We told them Dolly had run away. One asked what all the commotion the previous night had been about. I told them if they said anything about it they would lose their jobs."

"So why did you go after Lady Rose?" asked Kerridge.

"The newspapers implied she was holding something back. I was terrified. I went to see that villain, Bolton. When I visited him in prison, he told me he would do anything for money. I never thought at that time that I would have any use for him. But I needed him. The only gun we had was a lady's purse gun. I gave that to him.

"Then the temporary footman, Will, started blackmailing us. He had been awake during the night and had seen us carry a body into the carriage. I knew he would bleed us dry, so I called on him and finished him. That is all. You may release my parents."

"A charge of kidnapping and assault will be lodged against your father, but he will not hang. A statement will be typed for you to sign," said Kerridge.

When Jeremy was led out, Kerridge mopped his brow. "Thank God that's over. How is Lady Rose?"

"I have not had time to call on her."

"Then it's time you did. You don't know much about the ladies, do you?"

"Why do you say that?"

"You should not have called her a silly girl."

"I was upset, frightened for her."

"Better go and make your peace."

But when Harry called at the town house, he was told Lady Rose was "not at home."

That evening, he said to Becket, "I have offended Lady Rose, and Kerridge accuses me of not knowing anything about the ladies. How can I make amends?"

"There is such a thing as feminine curiosity," said Becket. "Lady Rose may be angry with you, but I am sure she would dearly like to know the outcome. May I suggest, sir, that you invite all of us involved in this case, even Phil and Miss Friendly and your secretary, to a luncheon party? You could hire a private room at Rules Restaurant."

Rules Restaurant was in Covent Garden. King Edward favoured it and had ordered a special staircase to be built in the restaurant so that he could escort his lady friends upstairs without being seen by the other diners.

"I'll do it," said Harry. "It is perfectly conventional for me to entertain a lady in a public restaurant, so her parents should have no objection."

Rose had suffered a blistering lecture and was told to stay in her rooms. She was not to leave the house. All her social engagements had been cancelled.

Harry knew that if he sent an invitation to his luncheon party, the earl would read it and might tear it up.

He decided to call in person.

The earl hummed and hawed about receiving him. Only the thought that Harry was after all still his daughter's fiancé and that he had saved her life made him reluctantly allow the captain to be shown up to the drawing-room.

"Well, what do you want?" asked the earl when Harry was ushered in.

The earl once again surveyed Harry's handsome and impeccably tailored figure. If only the wretched man hadn't chosen such an odd profession.

"Sit down, Cathcart. What now?"

Harry told him of Jeremy's confession. Then he said, "I know your daughter behaved dangerously, but it is thanks to her we caught him. But she certainly did not have my permission."

"If she had not met you, Rose would never have got into these scrapes."

"My lord, may I remind you that she was once about to be abused by a wastrel? That was none of my doing and you hired me to get her out of it. Nor was I responsible for her going to a suffragettes' meeting. Lady Rose will always need me to protect her."

The earl eyed him narrowly. "So when's the wedding?"

"We will soon fix a date."

"This engagement all seems fishy to me. Why are you here? To see Rose?"

"I am afraid your daughter is furious with me. I was so alarmed at her predicament and so frightened for her welfare that I called her a silly girl."

"And so she was."

"Lady Rose was very brave. I do not wish to be estranged from her. I am holding a private luncheon party in Rules for Lady Rose and some others. I hoped her curiosity about the outcome of the case would persuade her to accept the invitation. May I beg you to intercede on my behalf?"

The earl sat deep in thought. He wished with all his heart that the engagement could be broken off and that his wayward daughter would find someone more conventional. On the other hand, he shrewdly suspected Rose would run rings round a conventional husband to get her own way, and his wife had informed him that Rose was in love with Cathcart.

"All right. When?"

"Tomorrow at one o'clock. Miss Levine and Miss Friendly are invited as well."

"Levine's all right, but why invite the seamstress?"

"Because she was part of the investigation."

"Very well. I'll see what I can do."

After Harry had left, the earl went to the morning-room, where Lady Polly was lying on a chaise longue with her head in a book.

"Problem," said the earl. He told her about Harry's visit.

"I know my daughter has instructed the staff that she does not wish to see him," sighed Lady Polly, putting down her book.

"High-handed as ever. I've this ghastly feeling now that it's Cathcart or no one. We'll be stuck for her for life and I won't have an heir."

"I should think it is all very simple," said Lady Polly. "Tell her we do not wish her to go. She will immediately want to do the opposite. She always does."

———

They summoned Rose. She listened in silence. "Tell Captain Cathcart that I am not available."

"Quite right," said Lady Polly. "All the wretched man wants to do is to tell you what happened at Scotland Yard. But he has invited Friendly and Levine. I see no reason why they should not attend. In any case, you are being very sensible. I am sure you are just glad the nasty business is all over."

Rose bit her lip. She hated the idea of Daisy being told all the facts about the winding up of the case.

"Perhaps I should go," she said. "After all, I was the one who discovered the murderer for him."

"If you go, it will be against our express wishes," said her father.

Frustrated, Rose lost her temper. "Am I to be kept a prisoner in my rooms for the rest of my life? I tell you, I shall escape and find work. I have done it before and I can do it again."

"Oh, stop ranting," snapped the earl. "Go if you must."

Rose prepared herself with exceptional care for the luncheon. Normally she rebelled at the constrictions of undergarments to achieve the fashionable S-bend figure and wore only the minimum of petticoats and a light abbreviated corset. But she wanted to be armoured in high fashion, to show the wretched captain that she was a high-born lady and not the silly little girl he had claimed her to be.

Turner lashed her into a long corset of pink coutil—a tightly woven cotton fabric with a herringbone pattern—and put pads on her hips and under her arms. A pad went down the front to accentuate the bust and all to create the hourglass figure. Over that, after the silk stockings had been clipped to suspenders, went six petticoats, three of taffeta and three of organdy. Turner then held out a gown of pink taffeta and tulle and Rose dived into it and stood patiently while all the little buttons were fastened up the back.

She sat at the dressing-table while her hair was piled over pads, or "rats," as they were nicknamed. On top of her hair was placed a hat created by Miss Friendly, a cart-wheel of straw embellished with pink silk roses and tied round the brim with a pink silk ribbon with long streamers.

The dress had a high-boned collar to add to all the other constrictions.

Rose went gingerly down the stairs in her high heels.

Lady Polly came out of the drawing-room and surveyed her daughter. "I have never seen you look so fine. Such a welcome change from the tea-gowns you always seem to favour these days." Rose often preferred the tea-gown because it was a soft, filmy garment free from corsetry.

Miss Friendly and Daisy followed behind, equally corseted and hatted.

One of the earl's carriages took them to Rules in Covent Garden. They were ushered upstairs to the private dining-room booked by Harry.

"I think you know everyone," said Harry. He pulled up a seat for Rose and whispered, "I have never seen you look more beautiful."

Rose, who had dressed to impress him, was irrationally annoyed. Typical man, she thought. He only thinks I am beautiful when I am dressed like a doll.

Rose was sitting next to Harry at a round table. Daisy was placed next to Becket, Miss Friendly next to Phil, who had secretary Ailsa on his other side.

"I ordered a round table because this is an informal party,"

Harry began. "I am sure you are all anxious to hear what happened at Scotland Yard. But I think I should wait until the end of the meal when the waiters are dismissed."

Rose envied the ease of Daisy, chattering animatedly to Becket, and Miss Friendly seemed to be getting along famously with Phil. Ailsa drank steadily, smiling all around but not contributing much to the conversation.

The meal was lavish. Consommé was followed by trout fillets. Then quail cutlets followed by ham. After that roast ortolans, followed by asparagus. For the still hungry there was a desert of Gâteau Punch au Champagne, followed by anchovies on toast.

The food was delicious, but Rose was constricted, literally and metaphorically, from eating very much. Each mouthful seemed to tighten her stays even more and the close presence of Harry was taking away her appetite. He did not seem to notice her silences but kept up a flow of conversation about the weather, about the government and the fear of strikes. Only when he asked her about her charity work did Rose forget about her animosity towards him and become animated.

She told him again about her desire to set up a charity as soon as she reached her majority. She described how her work in the soup kitchen made her feel less useless and described some of the down-and-outs.

When the meal was finished and the waiters had been dismissed, Harry rapped a knife on his wineglass and said, "I can now tell you what happened."

They listened with rapt attention while he told them of Jeremy's confession. "The whole family was driven mad with ambition and snobbery," said Harry finally. "And yet, if it had not been for Lady Rose, I might not have had enough for a cast-iron case."

"What about Lord Berrow?" asked Daisy. "I'm amazed he had nothing to do with it."

"He did send someone to try to kill Miss Bridge," said Harry. "But he and Banks were killed in a motoring accident in Scotland, so they will not be troubling anyone again. I will never forget the bravery of our excellent Miss Bridge. Miss Bridge?" He realized he was looking at an empty seat.

"She's under the table, guv," said Phil, bending down.

"It's all my fault," said Harry contritely. "Please help her up. She is a missionaries' daughter and I don't think she is used to anything stronger than water."

Becket and Phil hoisted Ailsa up. She opened her eyes and smiled sleepily. "Whash goin' on?" she asked and slumped again.

"Becket, you had better take her down to the motor and take her home. Do you know the address?"

"Been there once," said Becket. "I'd better take Miss Levine with me. Need a lady along."

"Very well. I think we should all go. You have your carriage, Lady Rose?"

"Yes, a waiter will tell the coachman to come round."

"Then I will escort you and Miss Friendly to your home. Phil, you go with Becket and he can drive you to Chelsea after you leave Miss Bridge at her lodgings."

Harry helped Rose down from the carriage outside the town house. "Go indoors, Miss Friendly. I wish to have a word in private with my fiancée."

He turned to Rose and smiled into her eyes. "Are we friends again?"

"I think so."

He shielded their faces with his silk hat and bent to kiss her. At that very moment, a steel in Rose's corset which had gradually been working its way loose, stabbed her viciously and, as his mouth was about to meet hers, she winced.

To Harry, it looked like a wince of disgust.

He crammed his hat on his head. "Good day to you," he said, and he turned and strode off across the square.

Harry had been celibate for a long time. As he walked angrily through the streets of London in the direction of Chelsea, he cursed himself for ever having entered into an engagement with such as Lady Rose Summer. She was beautiful, yes, but she was as cold as ice.

Halfway home, he changed his mind and set off to The Club. It was always known simply as The Club and was considered less stuffy than White's or Brooks's.

He entered the coffee-room and was greeted by a tall figure. "Good God, old man, is it really you? I thought you had been killed at Magersfontein!"

Harry's face lightened as he recognized Colonel Jimmy Frent-Winston. Jimmy now looked like a rakish man-about-town. He had a high aquiline profile and bold blue eyes. "Sit down, Harry," he said. "Let's have a bottle of champagne."

"Still in the army?" asked Harry.

"Home on leave. Want to kick up my heels a bit. You're engaged, I hear."

"Not working out," said Harry, suddenly wanting to confide in someone.

"Ah, well, take my advice and cut and run."

They drank champagne and swapped war stories as the day drew on towards evening.

"I say," said Jimmy. "I know just the thing to end the day. Let's go to The Empire and find ourselves a pair of dazzlers."

The Empire music hall, a dream of blue and gold, was a most luxurious place. But its main attraction was the Promenade. The Promenade was where the aristocrats of prostitution paraded: blondes, brunettes and redheads, moving with a sort of feline grace and all with excellent manners. They never accosted a man; at the most he might feel the touch of a hand against his or the faint pressure of a silk-clad body as he stood at the rail watching the show below. As they moved to and fro, their jewels glittered and their silks swished and they exuded the scent of frangipani or patchouli.

In 1894, their presence had been attacked by a Mrs. Ormiston Chant, crying "white slavery." She and her supporters battled long and hard, but the assault failed completely. All Mrs. Ormiston Chant achieved was to become the most popular guy at the next Fifth of November, where she was burnt in effigy.

Harry hesitated. His few liaisons had been with respectable women, none of them ever serious. But Rose had wounded his pride and, he felt, his manhood. Besides, he had drunk rather a lot.

They took a cab. Harry was glad of Jimmy's company. He had been working so hard that he had had little time for friends.

The Empire declared itself a club, and Jimmy insisted on paying the entrance fee. It was full as usual, presided over by the manager, Mr. Hitchins, who ejected the rowdy with one white kid glove on the culprit's shoulder. Most of the ejected simply went round to the side door and paid five shillings to get back in.

"We'll go straight to the Promenade," said Jimmy. "Oh, I do like shopping, don't you?"

That was when Harry felt a sober jolt go through his body. At heart, he was a romantic, and the whole business of picking up a prostitute suddenly seemed unbearably sordid.

He knew better than to voice such views. Jimmy had a loud voice, the "Hyde Park drawl," and Harry felt sure he would protest loudly enough to make them certain of attention.

He waited until Jimmy was chatting to a pretty redhead and quietly made his way down the stairs. Someone on the stage was singing "She Was Only a Bird in a Gilded Cage." Harry went on out into the street. A poster at the entrance was advertising the new attraction of The Singing Blacksmith. Harry paused for a moment. Could that possibly be Dolly's blacksmith's son? But the case was closed, so he went on his way.

He decided to walk home to clear his head and banish infuriating pictures of Rose which kept coming into his mind.

Then he remembered the seductive Mrs. Losse. He craved the company of a lady who would flirt with him and stir his senses.

Harry set out for Kensington. He was just approaching the pretty house in Launceston Place when he saw a very grand carriage coming down the street. He drew back into the shadows.

The carriage stopped outside Mrs. Losse's door. Harry heard a voice say, "I won't be needing you any more tonight," and the carriage moved on. A portly figure moved up the front steps and then turned as if aware of being watched.

There was a lamp over the door. Harry recognized the

heavy-lidded protruding eyes, the sensual mouth and the thick beard. He was smoking a cigar.

As Harry watched, the door opened. Mrs. Losse stood there.

King Edward turned back and entered the house.

Harry began to walk towards Chelsea. It struck him that he had been unkind to Becket. Just because he, Harry Cathcart, had been unlucky in love, there was no need to make Becket suffer. He would miss him, but Becket should have his chance to marry.

He would set Becket and Daisy up in some business and Phil could take over as manservant.

Rose did not hear anything from Harry and fretted, wondering what to do. She and her parents had been invited down to Mrs. Barrington-Bruce's country home at the weekend. An invitation had been issued to Harry as well, but he had not telephoned to say he would be joining them or to make any apology.

As they travelled to Mrs. Barrington-Bruce's, Rose was aware that Daisy was in a state of suppressed excitement. She kept taking out a letter and reading it over and over again.

"What's in the letter?" asked Rose.

"Later," said Daisy, flashing a warning look in the direction of Lady Polly.

Brum was the one who collected and delivered the servants' mail. Daisy, although she had been elevated to the rank of companion, still qualified as a servant in Brum's eyes, and so she received a letter from Becket unopened. Had it gone to the earl, he would most certainly have opened it and read it.

When they finally reached their destination and were shown to their rooms, Daisy waited until the maids had unpacked their clothes until she said to Rose, "I have the most wonderful news!"

"What's that?"

"Becket has received permission from the captain to marry me. He is going to set us up in business."

Rose looked at her in dismay. "You will be leaving me?"

"Yes, but you've got Turner," said Daisy, made cheerfully selfish by the good news. "Aren't you going to congratulate me?"

"Of course, Daisy. I am sad because I do not want to lose you."

"I'll be around. Oh, I did so hope the captain would come this weekend and bring Becket. What's up with the man?"

"It's my fault. He . . . he tried to kiss me and at that very moment a steel came loose in my corset and dug into me and I made a face and he stormed off in a temper."

"Then write to him and tell him what happened!"

"I cannot. Ladies do not talk about stays."

"Oh, for heaven's sakes, tell him you had a bad twinge of indigestion."

"He shouldn't have tried to kiss me anyway. It is an engagement in name only."

Daisy looked at her with concern. "If you go on the way you're going, you'll soon have no engagement at all. Off to India and without me. Don't be so stubborn. Write to him. Tomorrow's Saturday. You could catch the Saturday post."

Rose smiled. "I'll do it."

Before dinner, she sat down and wrote a simple apology, making it as light-hearted as she could.

Then she called Turner and the long slow process of getting changed and dressed for dinner began.

There were various other guests at dinner and Rose was seated next to a Major Guy Alexander, who rattled away pleasantly about all sorts of society gossip. He turned out to know Harry but did not comment on his absence.

After dinner, the ladies retired to the drawing-room to leave the gentlemen to their port.

The drawing-room was overheated and Rose quietly opened the French windows and let herself out onto the terrace. The dining-room was next to the drawing-room and she could hear the sound of laughter. Then she thought she heard Harry's name and moved along the terrace and stood listening. Major Alexander was talking.

"You were asking about Cathcart? I know why the sly dog isn't here."

"Why?" someone asked.

"Ran into Jimmy Frent-Winston this morning. Told me he and Cathcart had gone to The Empire to pick up some lovelies at the Promenade. He said when he turned round, Cathcart had obviously got himself a lady and cleared off. Fast worker, hey?"

Rose turned away and walked down the steps to the garden, her breathing shallow. She knew about the Promenade because the campaign to get it closed down had been in all the newspapers.

It struck her with more force than ever before that ladies such as herself were merely the toys of society and expected to behave as such and turn a blind eye when the men went philandering. They had to dress up in clothes as stiff, elaborate and formal as any Japanese geisha and sit around and look decorative. They were not supposed to have any strong views on anything. They certainly would never be allowed to vote.

And Harry Cathcart was just like other men. We read romances and dream of our knights in shining armour, she thought, and they don't exist. She knew her own father would not be outraged to hear of Harry's visit to the Promenade. It was something gentlemen did.

She went sadly back to the drawing-room and out and down to the hall, where her letter to Harry lay on a silver tray with others, waiting for the morning post. She had hidden it under the others in case her father saw it and decided to read it. She took it out and tore it into little pieces and put the pieces in her gold mesh reticule.

Rose felt very alone. Daisy would leave and all she would have was a fiancé who consorted with tarts.

As she walked slowly back up to the drawing-room, she felt she was moving alone in a world where there was no love.

In Nice, Peter Petrey lounged on the terrace of the Palace Hotel and looked dreamily out at the moon sending a silver path across the Mediterranean. He glanced fondly at Jonathan. He felt he had never been so happy and contented in all his life.

In his dressing-room at The Empire, Roger Dallow read the report of the arrest of Jeremy Tremaine over and over again. At last he put down the paper with a sigh, remembering running across the summer fields with Dolly. He was now married to a little chorus girl and he had put on weight.

Ailsa Bridge sat in an empty church and prayed. She had been beset by the horrors the night before where large spiders had come crawling out of the woodwork. She prayed and prayed and then rose stiffly to her knees and went back to her lodgings. She picked up two bottles of gin from the kitchen counter, opened them and poured them down the sink.

After the weekend, Harry received a curt summons to call on the earl. When he arrived, the wrathful earl demanded to know the reason for his behaviour. To fail to turn up at the weekend without an apology was a snub of the first order.

Harry pleaded sickness and apologized as best he could. The earl privately hoped the sickness was not caused by something nasty he had picked up at The Empire.

"You'd better see Rose and make your apologies to her as well."

Rose reluctantly entered the drawing-room and the earl left them alone together.

Rose was wearing a tea-gown made by the Italian dress designer Fortuny. It was a long straight garment of artfully pleated satin held at the neck and wrist and waist by strings of small iridescent shells.

"You asked to see me?" she said coldly. "Please sit down."

"I have come to offer my sincere apologies. I was not well."

Rose suddenly felt rage burning up inside her. She forgot all the rules about what ladies were not supposed to know or say and remarked coldly, "I trust your complaint was not syphilis."

"What did you say?"

"You heard me. If you consort with whores at The Empire, it could be dangerous to your health."

"Who told you that!"

"Does it matter?"

"For your information, I had drunk a lot and met an old army friend. He suggested we go to The Empire. I was furious at your coldness. I tried to kiss you and you wrinkled up your face in disgust. No, I left almost as soon as we had arrived. I do not go with prostitutes and never have. I know, it makes me unusual, but that is the truth."

Rose sat in silence. The clock ticked in the corner. The apple-wood fire crackled on the hearth and a rush of wind went round the house like a great sigh.

"I was going to write to you and explain," she said at last. "I was going to explain that my expression was caused by indigestion. Then I overheard the men talking in the dining-room about you going to the Promenade. I tore up the letter. I may as well tell you the truth. When you bent to kiss me, one of the steels in my corset had worked loose and jabbed into me."

Harry's harsh face broke into a smile. "Oh, my Rose, you are indeed an original."

He stood up and went over to her, took her hands in his and kissed them, one after the other. Then he raised her up and folded her in his arms.

Brum's voice came from the doorway. "My lord wishes to know if you would like some refreshment."

Harry released Rose. "Nothing, thank you." He whispered to Rose, "Later." Then he took his leave.

Rose felt like singing. It was all going to be all right after all.

The Shufflebottom family was in Scarborough that summer on their annual holiday. They sat in chairs on the beach and watched the children.

"I was thinking," said Sally, "Rose should have been around to see Frankie take his first steps."

"They've gone back to their grand life and Rose has nothing to fear any more. Why should she bother with the likes of us?"

Sally looked down the beach. "That do look like Rose and Daisy walking along."

"Can't be!"

Sally stood up and screwed up her eyes against the sun. "It is," she cried. "It's them!"

Rose ran forward and hugged Sally. "I thought you'd forgotten us," said Sally as Bert stood up and the children gathered around."

"We couldn't do that," said Rose. "My parents are visiting friends in Yorkshire and they agreed to let us travel to Scarborough for the day."

"Is the captain with you?" asked Bert.

"No, he had to go abroad on business."

"And took Becket with him," said Daisy.

They spent a happy afternoon with the family and then climbed back into the earl's coach.

"I wish they would come back," said Daisy.

Rose nodded, thinking of how much she had looked forward to seeing Harry again, only to receive a visit from Brigadier Bill Handy to inform her that Harry had been sent abroad on government business.

"I don't think Becket and I will ever get married," mourned Daisy.

If anything happens to Harry, thought Rose, I will definitely never marry. He makes every other man seem dull.

The carriage climbed up out of Scarborough onto the bleakness of the moors. The day grew darker.

Rose shivered. She had a superstitious feeling that there was trouble ahead.